ACKNOWLEDGMENTS

Derby Rotten Scoundrels is a dream of the members of the Ohio River Valley Chapter of Sisters in Crime. Elaine Munsch and Sandra Leonard conceived it in a thunderstorm during a car ride to a Magna Cum Murder conference in Muncie, Indiana. The book was given form regarding theme, title, and length by its creative coordinator, Beverle Graves Myers, and brought to initial reality by authors Kit Ehrman, Laura (Young) Guetig, Tamara Huber, Sandra Cerow Leonard, Jeffrey Marks, Beverle Graves Myers, Elaine Munsch, Pat Robertson, and Brenda Stewart. After being coddled by gatekeeper Rena Moses, it was nurtured by editor Jeffrey Marks.

We want to thank all of the kind people who generously gave us their time and expertise—particularly P. J. Coldren, Luci "The Poison Lady" Zahray, and Marcia Talley, those who first read the stories and encouraged us to include all of them in the book.

Although the Kentucky Derby and its exciting social activities inspired our stories, knowledge and support for our book came from all over the United States. Los Angeles Sisters in Crime members Esta Sullivan and Kris Neri answered a multitude of questions about anthologies and publishing from the perspective of an authors group. Marcia Talley from the Chesapeake area was very helpful, even before she read the stories. Sandra Tooley and Mary Welk from the Chicago vicinity were fonts of practical information and gave us the courage to think we could really produce a book.

Over the years, we have had many stimulating speakers who have imparted wisdom in a variety of mystery-related topics. From private investigations to the labyrinth of a criminal prosecution, or to the kitchen of a poison expert, or the mind of a serial killer, their insight was invaluable to our creative processes.

Authors Don Bruns, Bill Butler, Terence Faherty, Sara Hoskinson Frommer, and the Taylor twins, Barbara Taylor McCafferty and Beverly Taylor Herald, were especially encouraging.

Other members of the Ohio River Valley Chapter have offered wonderful support and assistance. They are Linda Y. Adkins, Stephanie Allison, Daryll Anderson, Jerilyn Anderson, Laurel Louise Anderson, Janice Arnow, Edmund August, Gina Campbell, Kimberly Colley, Jeanie Curry, Marlis Day, Joan DiMartino, Barbara Disborough, Brook Dyer, Sarah Glenn, Mary E. Hanse, Catherine Henderson, Rita Higgins-Meyers, Evelyn Horn, Elizabeth Kutak, Marcia Larkin, Carolyn Laufer, Gwen Mayo, Margaret McCarthy, Jessica Peers, Suzanne Peers, Victoria Rose, Martha Scott, Sheila Shumate, and Cheryl Stuck.

There have been so many people who contributed to our effort that we apologize to anyone whose name is omitted. Please know that your help was appreciated.

Above all, we must thank our families and friends who tolerated our writing absences only to have us emerge from in front of the computer to ask, "How does this sound?" Without them, there would be no *Derby Rotten Scoundrels*.

TABLE OF CONTENTS

Nothing stirs the imagination and excites the blood like a horse race. From impromptu races on Market Street in downtown Louisville in the late 1700s to the multimillion-dollar industry it is today, horse racing has long been an integral part of Kentucky's history.

When 26-year-old Colonel M. Lewis Clark created Churchill Downs in 1875 to showcase the Kentucky breeding industry, the Kentucky Derby was born. Over the years, the facility and the tradition have endured financial instability, various reform movements to abolish horse racing, the Great Depression and the Great Flood of 1937, numerous wars, and man's folly.

But some threats are less easily detected. In the summer of 1999, when a record heat wave baked the Eastern seaboard and shimmered off the streets of New York City some 785 miles from the stately twin spires at Churchill Downs, no one suspected the threat lurking in the murky waters surrounding Staten Island. But as the seasons passed, the threat of West Nile virus grew and spread westward, literally borne on a bird's wings.

Because the horse is highly susceptible to encephalitis, the industry sat up and took notice. A vaccine was developed, and as the virus crept across the border into Kentucky during the summer of 2001, numerous precautions were, and still are, being taken to minimize the threat to one of the state's most prestigious industries.

RETRIBUTION
by Kit Ehrman

Kit Ehrman is the author of At Risk *and* Dead Man's Touch. *Both mysteries are published by Poisoned Pen Press and feature Steve Cline, an amateur sleuth who works in the horse industry. Kit has worked as a groom, veterinary assistant, and barn manager at numerous horse facilities in Maryland and Pennsylvania and currently lives in Columbus, Indiana. To learn more about the series, check out* www.kitehrman.com.

"YOU'RE KIDDING, RIGHT?"

Gerrich gathered the papers together and tucked them in a file folder; then he looked at me over his gold-rimmed bifocals. "Since when have you known me to possess a sense of humor, Ramsey?"

One of Gerrich's gofers choked on his Coke. I looked at Nobbie. The corner of his mouth twitched as he stared steadfastly at the stretch of conference table before him.

"But I don't know a damn thing about horses," I said, "except you feed one end and clean up after the other."

"Agent Weiler assures me that even an idiot can handle the job."

I glanced at Weiler, whom I'd never met, then at Gerrich's right-hand man. He stood two paces behind his boss in a wide-legged stance, his hands clasped behind his back and a smirk on his face. His eyes sparkled with amusement, and it occurred to me that everyone in that room, except possibly for Weiler, knew why Gerrich was sticking me with this asinine assignment.

"Agent Noblitt," Gerrich told me, "will set up surveillance and run the van with help from the Louisville office. And you and Agent Weiler will work undercover in the barn."

Above my head, a fluorescent tube buzzed over the hum of the ventilation system. The cooled air slid across the back of my neck, yet my skin felt hot.

"But I don't look the part," I said, and it was true. I was a 35-year-old, six-two, 220-pound, clean-shaven white male with a buzz cut, and I'd spent most of those years working out in a gym.

"Weiler will help you blend in."

I looked across the table at her, and she stared right back, her expression composed and unreadable. Weiler was pretty and blonde and young. Early twenties. Refined bone structure under smooth honey-colored skin that glowed with health. Big blue intelligent eyes. Small ears that lay flat against her head, nice square shoulders, delicate hands. She'd pulled her hair into some kind of fancy braid at the back of her head; it must have taken her half an hour to do and would have taken me all week.

She'd been stationed at Quantico since joining the Bureau, and as far as I knew, she'd never worked in the field. This assignment was destined to fail, and I figured that's what Gerrich had in mind all along. One more screw up, and my career was in the toilet.

"Pick up the files on the way out," Gerrich ordered. "I expect you to be in position and set up, thirty-six hours, max. You've got thirteen days before the Kentucky Derby to neutralize the threat."

When Weiler stood and gathered the folders together, Nobbie jerked his chair back, and the two of us followed her into the hall. She led the way, which was fine by me. Her tailored suit snugged her hips and clung neatly to the curve of her thighs with each step she took down the corridor. And she had a nice ass, too.

We waited for the elevator, and in a moment, I felt a subtle vibration beneath my shoes as the car lumbered up the shaft and bumped to a halt on our floor with a muffled thud. Otherwise, the building was shrouded in a deep-seated quiet typical for a Sunday morning.

We rode the elevator down to the parking garage, and when the door slid open, air laden with the stale smell of exhaust and engine oil and grease swirled into the car and mingled with Weiler's perfume. Some kind of flower. Lilac, maybe. We stepped out, and Nobbie headed for the van.

"See you in Louisville," he said, winking at me.

"You've worked with Agent Noblitt before?" Weiler asked over her shoulder as we neared the motor pool, and I figured she was just making small talk until we could get down to business.

"Yeah. Six years and counting. And let's drop the 'agent' bit. It gets old. Everybody calls him Nobbie. I'm Jack."

She nodded, then walked behind the row of dark-colored Crown Vics and Caprices parked along the west wall. Each one was outfitted with your basic government-issue, nondescript hubcaps and four antennas sticking out of the trunk. Nothing any self-respecting criminal would miss.

"I'm Maggie," she said.

"Well, Maggie. Mind if we stop by my place before we head south?"

"That was my intention." She unlocked a black Crown Vic, tossed the folders on the backseat, and slid behind the wheel. "You own some ratty jeans and T-shirts?"

I folded myself into the sedan and ratchetted the passenger's seat back as far as possible. "How ratty?"

"Work worn. Maybe some holes. And you'll need a couple flannel shirts, in case it gets cold. And work boots."

"O-k-a-y," I said slowly, and she rolled her eyes.

We stopped at my apartment just off Sheridan Road and a stone's throw from the U.S. Naval Training Center on the west shore of Lake Michigan. Home wasn't much, really. Just a cramped one-bedroom over a garage, with a combination kitchen/sitting room and a bath tucked under the eaves. But it suited me. I grabbed some gear out of the bathroom, while Maggie rooted through my clothes like she owned the place.

When I came out, she was sitting by the window, gazing at the horizon over the lake. She'd taken off her jacket, and her soft nylon blouse clung to her breasts and the small of her back. Everything about her looked soft and feminine, except for the Glock slotted into her waistband.

"Ready?" I asked.

She nodded, then we headed to the car. Three hundred twenty-nine point two miles south to Louisville. Once we hit I-65, I used the drive to study the case file.

On March 20, Daniel Lahaye, a highly respected racehorse trainer, had been ordered by an unknown subject—officially designated UNSUB—to scratch his Derby runner, Watercourse. If he didn't comply, the UNSUB would infect his entire stable with a vaccine-resistant strain of West Nile virus, a mosquito-borne disease that often proves fatal to birds and horses. Shortly thereafter, as a demonstration of his ability to carry out the threat, the UNSUB called Lahaye and told him his stable pony had been infected. The blood test came back positive, and the pony was euthanized that very morning.

All of which got us exactly nowhere. The UNSUB had been smart enough to use a pay phone. The surrounding neighborhood had been canvassed. Nearby security cameras had been examined, but the UNSUB conveniently hadn't been caught on film. There'd been no witnesses. No leads to follow, whatsoever.

Since racketeering falls under federal jurisdiction, the Thoroughbred Racing Protective Bureau had almost immediately asked the FBI for help. However, thanks to the upcoming Derby, both the LPD and FBI were stretched thin, but they were handling it.

And then the stakes escalated to murder.

It took two days for Louisville to make the connection, which wasn't bad. They cross-referenced employee records, searching for a link between a track employee and someone who worked in a lab and would conceivably have access to the virus, but they had yet to come up with a match. That all changed when a technician at Lindsay Pharmaceuticals in Frankfort was found stuffed in the trunk of his car with a fatal stab wound to the chest. A flare may as well have been set off, for all the excitement it generated. He had easy access to the virus. Now we just had to link him to someone at the track, but so far, nothing had panned out.

"So," I said, "how in the hell do you infect a horse with this disease, anyway?"

Maggie shrugged. "As long as you have access to the virus, it'd be simple. Just inject the horse in the muscle is all. Nothing to it."

"But doing it in a training barn without getting caught?"

She shook her head. "Racehorses get injections all the time. They're used to it. They're also used to biting flies, and the injection wouldn't feel much different. It's not like you'd have to give them a large dose. One cc would be enough. That small of an amount, you could use a 3-cc syringe and inject it one-handed. The needle pricks the skin, and you depress the plunger in one quick motion. No one would realize what you've done. If the horse jumps, well, he's just edgy, that's all."

I thought about it for a moment and considered how to guard against that kind of threat, then decided that unless something opened up with the Frankfort lead, and we discovered who was behind the threat, my career inched closer to the sewer with each passing mile.

"Stopping them will be impossible," I observed.

"Maybe."

"I should be in Frankfort, chasing down leads. That's something I'm damned good at. Stuck in the barn, I'll effectively be out of the loop."

"Not true." She glanced at me, then looked back at the road. Her slim hand was relaxed on the steering wheel, her grip light.

I checked the speedometer. She'd set the cruise control at 78 as soon as we'd cleared Crown Point.

"The guy in Frankfort gave the virus to someone, and that someone's in Louisville." She flexed her right foot, and her calf muscles tightened under her nylons. "What does Gerrich have against you, anyway?"

I rubbed my face. "We worked a kidnapping together, and, simply put, I got the kid back but blew up Gerrich's car in the process."

"So?"

"Not his pool car," I said. "His personal car. A '69 Porsche."

She whistled under her breath and asked if I was as clueless about horses as I claimed to be.

"Well, I've seen them in parades," I said. "From a distance."

Maggie tapped her nails on the steering wheel, then told me what my undercover job at the track would entail. Apparently I would be hot-walking, whatever the hell that meant. She described the layout of a training barn, then gave me a brief overview of equine psychology. In particular, she wanted me to understand what I should do if one of the horses spooked, but I figured it all came down to confidence and control, like everything else.

"Jack," she said, glancing at me, "they outweigh you by eight hundred pounds. You can't overpower them, so you've got to out-think them."

"That shouldn't be too hard."

She shook her head. "Just be careful, and if you have any questions, ask."

By 1400 hours, we'd been briefed by Louisville's Assistant Special Agent in Charge and two guys who'd driven in from the resident agency in Frankfort. On our way out, we picked up track ID badges that would get us through security. As we turned off Martin Luther King Jr. Place, Weiler flipped open her cell phone and arranged to meet Lahaye at his barn later in the day, then she detoured east onto I-64.

"Where're we going?"

"Props and a little instruction," she said. "We can't do this job driving around in a Crown Vic."

"And just what do you mean by 'instruction'?"

Maggie grinned. "You'll see."

Thirty-six miles out, she exited I-64 and headed south on State Road 53. Just past Mt. Eden, she hung a left and bumped the sedan onto a gravel drive that led to a ranch of sorts.

"I grew up here," she said. She introduced me to her aunt and uncle, then told me to change into work clothes and meet her in the barn.

Seven minutes later, I slid the barn door open and stepped into a large area stacked with hay. About the size of a cathedral, it was dark except for a couple of shafts of sunlight that cut through gaps in the wood siding and puddled on the floorboards. Dust particles moved lazily through the air, and high above my head, a pigeon fluttered its wings.

"Maggie?"

"I'm downstairs. Go back outside and walk down the path to your left."

As I rounded the corner, Maggie led a big brown horse out of the lower portion of the barn. I held up and watched her from a distance.

She wore cowboy boots and a checked cotton shirt tucked into snug blue jeans, and the transformation from FBI to country girl was astounding and incredibly sexy.

When she looked up at me, her gaze fixed on my waist, and she grinned. I glanced down as she said, "What? Are you going to shoot him if he doesn't listen?"

Out of habit, I'd hooked my badge and 9 mm Glock on my belt. "You never know. It might come in handy."

"Come on. I'll teach you how to lead him."

I stepped alongside the horse's left shoulder as directed, then Maggie placed my right hand on the leather strap just below a chain that ran across the horse's nose. She stood close, stretched out the excess leather, and pressed it into my left hand. Her fingers were light on my skin, and the scent of her perfume hung in the air between us. I gazed down at her as she frowned in concentration, making sure my grip was correct.

She taught me how to position my body as I led the horse and turned him in both directions before leading him through narrow stall doorways. She showed me how to hold him still for baths, how to jiggle the chain to make him pay attention, and how to jerk on his lead if he misbehaved.

After I passed Equine Mobility and Control Techniques 101, Maggie pulled a rusted-out GMC pickup from a garage bay. Our undercover vehicle, I assumed. I climbed into the Crown Vic, jammed the driver's seat all the way back, and followed her to Churchill Downs, where Lahaye had a barn.

Three blocks from the track, I smelled the horses—an earthy, pungent odor that seemed totally out of place in the middle of a city, in the same way that I'd always thought zoos smelled when I was a kid.

Dan Lahaye was a handsome man in his late fifties. He was almost as tall as me, big-boned and fit, with brown hair going gray round the temples. And he was worried.

He seemed distracted as he showed us around, pointing out the feed room and tack room. We passed a guard sitting outside one of the stalls, and I spotted pinhole cameras under the eaves in each corner of the barn. Lahaye led us into his office, where another guard sat at a desk, and I noted the accompanying monitor and VCR on a credenza behind him. Lahaye introduced us.

We exchanged pleasantries, then I asked Lahaye, "You only have four cameras set up?"

He nodded.

"Who monitors them?"

"The security firm I hired, and there's a lead that transmits the feed to a house just the other side of the road where you guys are set up."

I rubbed the back of my neck. "We'll be adding more cameras in the next couple days."

He shrugged. "Anything you want."

I'd planned on tapping Lahaye's phone if it wasn't already. I would ask Nobbie to wire the entire barn for sound, plus all the nearby restrooms used by track employees. Then we'd look into tapping the pay phones around the barns.

"Let me show you Watercourse," he said.

I had to admit, the horses I'd seen so far weren't all that impressive, and Watercourse was no exception. He was sleek enough, like the others; but based on my extensive equine knowledge after watching a few minutes of Derby coverage on television, I'd expected him to be taller and more substantial in the flesh.

Watercourse was standing at the back of his stall, with his head held low and his eyes half closed. When the colt saw Lahaye, he made a low sound in his throat and fluttered his nostrils, then he crossed the stall and poked his head into the aisle.

The trainer pulled a chunk of carrot out of his pocket, then cupped his hand under the horse's nose. The animal sucked the carrot into his mouth without hesitation and champed down with his massive jaws. I'd've been checking my fingers if I'd done that.

"Can you afford another guard?" I asked as I listened to the horse grind his teeth, no doubt mashing the carrot to mush. His chewing was loud and hollow-sounding.

Lahaye shook his head. "Two's bad enough."

"Were all these precautions in place when the pony was infected?"

He paused. "That's hard to say. Since we couldn't determine how long the virus had been in the gelding's system, he may have been infected before the initial phone call."

I nodded. "Maybe the pony was all he could manage. If that's the case, the perp might not be able to make good on his threat."

"Yeah, but what if he can?"

I walked around the barn once more before Maggie and I drove to the house the FBI had rented on Longfield Avenue. This time she followed me.

She pulled into a parking space behind the Crown Vic, and as she climbed out, I said, "I don't get it. What do you do with ponies at a racetrack?"

"The 'ponies' are really horses. The horses that lead or *pony* the racehorses around the track are called ponies."

"Okay." I grabbed my gear out of the trunk. "This oughta be real fun."

Maggie rolled her eyes and hefted her suitcase onto the pavement.

"How do you know so much, anyway?" I asked.

"I used to gallop racehorses when I was in college."

I let my gaze drift over her slender build, and she picked up on my doubt.

"Finesse, Jack. It's all about finesse. You can't overpower them." She grinned and gave me the once-over, just as I'd done. "Not even you."

In the living room, a young guy from the Louisville office fiddled with a lead behind a split-screen monitor. I drew a diagram of the barn and told Nobbie where I wanted him to set up additional surveillance.

After we ate Chinese carryout, we worked out the sleeping arrangements. The Louisville crew had confiscated the first-floor bedroom, which left three upstairs. Maggie took the master bedroom with a private bath, leaving a twin bed in a back bedroom and a large front bedroom with a full-size bed.

Nobbie and I flipped for it, and I got the twin. "Just wonderful," I grumbled.

Maggie grinned and told me to get a good night's sleep, then she closed her door.

I made the mistake of staying up and rereading the files, paying particular attention to the Frankfort file, so when my watch alarm chirped at 0400 hours, I snapped it off and rolled onto my back. The next thing I knew, Maggie was shaking my shoulder.

"Wake up, Jack. Time to get to work."

I groaned, then came fully awake as Maggie spun on her heels and headed for the door. I glanced down to be sure that I hadn't kicked off my sheet during the night, then I fumbled into my clothes and picked up my Glock. I couldn't very well carry it around the barn, so I tucked it under the mattress and dug the ankle holster out of my duffel. I checked the load in the Baretta, then latched it around my left ankle and yanked my pant leg down. As I double-checked that my knife was in my pocket, Maggie rapped on the door.

Fifteen minutes later, Maggie shuttled us over to the track, and I started my first day as a hot-walker. An elderly black man, with hunched shoulders and a tic working the skin by his left eye, gave me my first horse. If that old guy could handle these horses, I didn't have anything to worry about, despite my inexperience. I walked the first one without any trouble, fifteen loops around the barn.

He was a good-sized white horse with black flecks over his

entire body. His head nodded as he walked, and it took me a lap or two to get used to his rhythm. He seemed to watch me out of the corner of his eye, and I had the distinct impression that he knew I hadn't a clue what I was doing.

I had a short break before my next horse, so I stood by the tack room door and watched. The backside, as I'd learned the barn area was called, was busier that I'd anticipated. A constant stream of people and horses came and went. And there were a lot of outsiders milling about. Press, owners, and anyone who could bluff their way through the gate. None of it good for security.

Maggie came around the corner, leading a brown horse that already wore a saddle and bridle. She passed by without looking in my direction.

My next horse, an orange-colored filly named Thursday's Secret, ground her teeth the entire time, and I could hardly wait to be rid of her. Her blue-brown eyes were stretched wide, and she had this annoying habit of leaning into me. I'd push her off, and in three strides, her shoulder would be pressed against mine.

I managed to get through the day's work without making any obvious blunders. I was tired, and my shoulder hurt from holding my arm out for six hours straight.

"How're you doing?" Maggie asked when I met her in the parking lot.

"Great, and you?"

"I'm beat."

Seven days later, I'd grown used to the routine and probably knew more about everyone in the barn than their own mothers. Countless times I'd studied the background checks and surveillance records provided by the Louisville guys, and all of it had added up to a big fat zero. We hadn't heard a peep from the UNSUB, either, and that bothered me.

I scooped the fast-food wrappers into the trash and walked into the living room. The porch windows glowed red as the sun slid toward the horizon.

"The guy can't deliver," I said. "He's just jerking Lahaye around."

"We can't count on that." Maggie was sprawled on the sofa with a can of Diet Coke balanced on her stomach. She was wearing a pair of turquoise shorts, and her slim, tanned legs were crossed at the ankles.

Nobbie's surveillance tapes had uncovered a lot of unscrupulous behavior that the Thoroughbred Racing Protective Bureau would find interesting, but nothing led back to our guy.

I sat down and closed my eyes. "Who benefits?"

"What?"

"Who benefits from stopping Watercourse?"

"About a gazillion people. Anybody who wants another horse to win the Derby."

"Okay." I propped my feet on the coffee table. "But who benefits if Lahaye's stable is infected with West Nile?"

She shrugged.

"No one, Maggie. Not from a race-fixing standpoint. If our UNSUB's serious, then his goal is personal and aimed solely at hurting Lahaye." I stood up. "It's about time we investigated Mr. Daniel S. Lahaye."

I picked up the phone and punched in the number for the Louisville office. Once I set the wheels rolling, we turned in for the night.

By 0800 hours Tuesday, the backside was hopping. A TV van slid into a parking spot near the end of the barn, and anyone who could worm their way through the gate apparently had— from the press and their photographers to owners and their friends. All the traffic complicated security, and I was thankful I'd been able to talk Lahaye into hiring another guard.

The horses were on edge, too. I led a bay filly down the

shedrow, and as we neared the corner, a fashionably dressed couple stepped out of the trainer's office, followed by Lahaye himself. The man turned toward the exit. As he did so, Lahaye placed his hand on the woman's back, as if to guide her, but there was an element of intimacy to the gesture as well. She looked over her shoulder at him, and her expression was anything but platonic.

I ID'd the couple easily enough, and during my break, I requested a full report on them. The Louisville office faxed a preliminary write-up to the house, and it was lying on the kitchen table when we returned at 1100 hours. I scanned the report and handed it to Maggie.

Chester and Mary Jordan had been married twenty years. They lived in Lexington, where he worked as an investment banker. He owned a dozen or so horses, two of which were stabled in Lahaye's barn.

Maggie dropped the file onto the table. "Mary has a lot of time on her hands, doesn't she?"

I requested Jordan's phone records for the past six months and asked the Louisville office to cross-reference his name with the Frankfort murder victim. Then we waited.

A full report came in around midnight, with the most damning information listed first.

Chester Jordan's bank had financed an expansion at Lindsay Pharmaceuticals in the mid-nineties, which required numerous tours on Jordan's part. In all probability, he knew the vic. And judging by the phone records, Mary Jordan knew Lahaye very well, indeed.

"Let's go," I said.

Maggie raised her eyebrows. "Now?"

"Middle-of-the-night interrogations can be extremely effective. They catch the perps off guard. Plus, we wait for morning, we'll have ten guys from the Louisville office tagging along."

Fifty minutes later, Maggie pulled into a circular drive in front of a huge Victorian and killed the lights.

"Nice to be rich, ain't it?" I said.

"Oh, I don't know. All this"—Maggie waved her hand—"wasn't enough to keep Mary happy, now, was it?"

"Apparently not."

We got out of the car and let the doors click shut, then I slipped on my nylon jacket with FBI silk-screened across the back in six-inch-high reflective letters. I touched the gun on my hip and noticed that Maggie had done the same.

"You okay?" I whispered and saw her nod.

She rang the doorbell, and after a minute, we heard footsteps in the foyer.

"Who's there?"

"FBI, Mr. Jordan," I said.

He opened the door and squinted at us as we held up our badges. "What do you want?"

"May we come in?" I asked.

He glanced from me to Maggie, then he led us into a sitting room off the main hall.

I'd always found that the most direct approach generated the best results, so I said, "Mr. Jordan, where were you on the night of April 15th?"

"Huh?"

"Tuesday night, Mr. Jordan. April 15th? You know, tax day?"

"I don't remember."

"We have reason to believe that on that night, at approximately nine-thirty, you met Alexander Wetzel in the parking lot of Lindsay Pharmaceuticals."

I thought Jordan was going to pass out right then and there. His skin blanched, and he swayed on his feet.

I grabbed his elbow and steadied him. "Have a seat, Mr. Jordan, and tell us what happened."

He stumbled backward in his bedroom slippers and flopped into a heavily cushioned chair, which was perfect from a security standpoint. He'd be just a tad slower getting to his feet. I Mirandized him, and then repeated my question.

"I . . . eh . . . I. . . ." His voice faltered, and he wouldn't meet my eyes.

"It's all right, Mr. Jordan," I said, and then I played a hunch. "He was going to blackmail you, wasn't he?"

Jordan folded his hands in his lap and nodded, as a tear slid down his cheek and rolled off his chin. "When he found out what I really wanted the virus for, that I didn't actually have a huge race-fixing scheme in place that he could get rich from, he was furious. Said he'd report me. Then I guess he thought better of it, because he'd implicate himself, doing that. The next thing I know, he's calling me up, demanding money."

Jordan inhaled sharply, and mucus rattled in his sinuses. "I was actually going to pay him, you know? But he said it wasn't enough. He wanted more, and I . . . I just lost it."

"That's understandable, Mr. Jordan. Where do you have the virus?"

He jerked his head toward a small refrigerator sitting on the floor alongside a desk. Maggie crossed the room and opened the door.

As so often happens, once they make a confession, they keep going, and Jordan was no exception.

"I wanted to hurt Lahaye so bad after I found out about the two of them, I figured the best way to accomplish that was to take his horses away, then he'd understand how it feels to lose what you love most in this world."

"I can't find it," Maggie said, and I looked at her as she straightened and turned toward us. Her eyes widened, and in the same instant, Jordan squawked.

I pivoted around as Mrs. Jordan lunged at her husband and

brought her hand down in a sweeping arc toward his chest. I grabbed her wrist before she made contact. Something narrow and milky white dropped on the carpet.

We cuffed them both, then Maggie gingerly picked up the little syringe with an inch-long needle sticking out of one end. "You okay, Jack?"

"Never been better."

"Inside the thunder." That's how jockey Laura Jean describes sitting on a 1200-pound Thoroughbred, waiting for the starting gate to open. Male or female, a jockey must be among the fittest of all athletes. Galloping stirrup-to-stirrup at speeds that leave no room for mistake, a jockey must show focus, courage, and an exceptional finesse in communicating with horses.

Most jockeys train on the job, starting as hot-walkers or exercise riders and going on to ride as apprentices. Once they turn professional, jockeys tend to lead a nomadic life, depending on agents to find mounts at racetracks in states where they are licensed to ride. Only a few reach the top rank where riding a Kentucky Derby contender is possible.

It's a challenging profession. Days start early and may hold five to six races, weight must be strictly maintained, and career-ending injuries are common. But at the end of the day, how many people can say they've galloped inside the thunder?

DEAD HEAT WITH A PALE HORSE

by Beverle Graves Myers

Beverle Graves Myers writes mystery, fantasy, and horror from her home in Louisville, Kentucky. Her short stories have appeared in Woman's World *and* Futures *and online at Flashquake, Orchard Press Mysteries, Shred of Evidence, and Fables.*

BURY MY HEART—spooky name for a filly that came close to laying me out for good. I rode her during the first week of Churchill Downs' Spring Meet. It was a stakes race with a nice purse, but nothing compared to the upcoming Kentucky Derby. The Derby was the granddaddy of them all, the big one that every jock dreamed of winning.

Thanks to a night of pelting rain, the track was as sloppy as I'd ever seen in my fifteen years on the circuit. I was up for it, but Bury My Heart was no mudder. Before we even made it to the starting gate, she started mincing around like her precious hooves were sinking in molasses. Still, she broke from the gate with the rest of the field, and I managed to settle her back in sixth place for the first half-mile.

Peering through two layers of mud goggles, I could barely make out Churchill's famous twin spires against the smudgy slate sky, but I heard the screaming crowd in the grandstands well enough. Somebody up front was making a move; the lead horses angled out five wide, leaving a narrow hole on the rail. I pulled down my top pair of slush-spattered goggles. If Bury My Heart would cooperate, I could drive her clean through.

The filly balked. She'd had it with sloshing through goo and just wanted to sit tight. I leaned forward, chirping and cooing in her left ear, but she wasn't having any of my sweet talk.

Suddenly, a big gray was bearing in on us from the outside. I didn't recognize him. I made it a practice to know every horse in every race I rode, but this one had slipped by me. He was on the muscle, driving down the lane so smoothly that I wondered if his hooves even touched the track. As he blew past, I saw that the jock wore solid red with a black ace of spades centered on his back.

I squinted through goggles rapidly turning opaque with gobs of flying muck. Whose freakin' silks were those?

It must have started raining again. The big gray's flanks glistened like giant pearls streaming with iridescent droplets, and what should have been the homestretch had become a swirling wall of blue-green mist. A watery roar filled my ears.

With my heart hammering against my ribs, I pulled down my last pair of goggles. That was better—sunshine!

But the lead horses had disappeared, and I wasn't at Churchill anymore.

I was five years old, dressed in a cowboy outfit, guiding a broomstick hobbyhorse around a backyard oval that Mom had laid out with porch furniture and crepe paper. Bobbing yellow balloons marked the finish line.

I was galloping my stick like I could blow a hole in the wind, but the pale gray and his scarlet-clad rider crowded me, matching me stride for stride. I strained forward, desperate to cross the finish line, but those yellow balloons wouldn't get any closer. The gray and I were in a dead heat that promised to last forever.

Whimpering in frustration, I stole a look at the jock on my

rival. He rode low in the irons, face nearly buried in his horse's luminous mane, back hunched into a bony parabola. With a latch-like click, his face swiveled toward me. Bug-eyed mud goggles slithered up his bleached, domed forehead. His toothy death's-head grin was the last sight I saw before Bury My Heart's half-ton carcass rolled over my 108-pound frame.

I woke up at University Hospital—long about the end of May. I had only scattered memories of its award-winning trauma unit and the tedious surgeries that had saved my life, but I was getting to know its orthopedic rehab floor real well.

My first visitor after I'd returned to the rational world was my agent, Jimmy Dobbins. His ever-present baby-blue windbreaker was a sight for sore eyes, but I didn't like the nervous expression on his round face.

"Matt LeMaster. . . ." He said my name like he was reading my obituary, then he shook his head. "I never would've thought it of you. I always had you pegged for a good guy."

"What are you talking about, Jimmy?" I *was* a good guy. Well, at least not too bad. I'd certainly encountered worse during my years of knocking around stables and racetracks.

He shuffled awkwardly and set a bunch of wilted posies on the nightstand by my bed. I mashed my thumb on the button that raised my top half. My lower half was immobile, connected to a contraption of pins and pulleys that kept my shattered right tibia exactly where the doctors wanted it. "What is it?" I repeated over the whirr of the bed's machinery.

"Sorry to let you have it like this." My old buddy sighed. "You'll get the official papers in the mail, but I thought you deserved a heads up. The Racing Commission met while you were still out. You're suspended."

I jerked upright, wincing as my leg pulled at its harness. "Suspended for what? Spilling on a sloppy track?"

"Don't kid me, Matt. You know that's not it. You tested positive. When you rode Bury My Heart, you were on some kind of dope that I can't even pronounce."

"No way! You know I don't do drugs. Never have, never will."

"The lab tests say different. They repeated them several times to make sure." He reached in the pocket of his windbreaker for a crumpled paper. "I wrote it down. It's an indole . . . alkaloid . . . something." He handed the slip over. "Here, it's kind of like what the kids call 'acid.'"

I looked up at the agent who'd kept me in mounts for the better part of ten years. Did Jimmy really believe that I'd risk my own safety, plus my horse and the other riders for a trip to La-La Land? The down-turned mouth that almost met his wobbly chins gave me my answer.

"I'm going to fight the suspension," I said through clenched teeth.

"You'll face an uphill battle . . . seeing as the horse had to be put down and everything."

As if I couldn't remember Bury My Heart's braying screams tearing at my ears. "All the more reason," I replied.

He nodded sadly, then nodded his head toward my smashed leg. "Does it really matter?"

"Consider this a temporary setback. Bones heal, you know, if you give them enough time. The physical therapist puts me through my paces twice a day. I do everything she tells me and more beside, but. . . ." I hesitated. "But if it turns out that I can't ride again, I'm going out clean, not with a drug charge hanging over my head."

I thought about Jimmy's bombshell for most of the afternoon. A jockey's success and survival depend on his capacity to make split-second decisions and convince a large, galloping animal to carry them out. Any substance that messed with his head could be lethal. I hadn't taken anything to cause the weird vision I'd experienced on Bury My Heart, so where had the dope come from?

I was ready with plenty of questions when the physical therapist showed up for my afternoon torture session. Teri O'Callahan was a tiny strawberry blonde with enough upper-body strength to handle a bolting Thoroughbred. Her uniform was a loose, green scrub top over white pants just tight enough to let the flowers on her panties show through. She hadn't been working with me long, but when someone drives you to the limits of your pain threshold on a daily basis, you get to know him or her fast.

"Matt, you should really ask your doctor these questions," she said as she studied the paper Jimmy had left with me.

"You mean that prune-faced guy who leads around the bunch of white coats and lectures about me like I'm deaf, dumb, and blind?"

She couldn't resist a sympathetic smirk.

"Here's the deal, Teri, I'm stuck in this bed and don't know much about this stuff, anyway. I was probably hanging around the barn while you were getting A's in chemistry. I need you to find out what this drug looks like and how long it takes to work."

Even if she'd said no, she earned my undying affection for believing in me, for not once asking if maybe I hadn't fooled around with some pills or something. But she didn't turn me down.

She came back the next morning with a book and a folder of old class notes. "Looks like the basement chemists are ahead of the textbooks on this one." She propped the open book up on my raised thigh and leaned over to point a businesslike finger at a long string of numbers and letters. "This is the closest thing I could find. It's the formula for an indole derivative. Any reasonably smart kid who's taken organic chemistry could whip some up, but in nature, it comes from a plant in the morning glory family. The Aztecs used to grind the seeds and make a tea to use in their sacred rituals."

"What does it do?"

"It causes hallucinations. The Aztec shamans thought they were flying through the air, going on vision quests."

I shook my head. Half of my mind was on the alluring cleft in her green scrub top and the other half on the pharmacology book. I thumbed through pages of small type and chemical formulas. "I'll never get through all of this. Let's cut to the chase. I don't drink morning glory tea, so how'd this drug get in my head?"

She moved to unpack the ankle weights that would give my good leg a workout. "You ingested it somehow—in food or liquid. Probably an hour or so before you started hallucinating. Can you remember what you put in your mouth that morning?"

While I raised and lowered my weighted leg, I tried to picture the morning of the spill. "Like usual," I told her, "I woke up before dawn. There's no kitchen at my place—I just rent a motel room wherever I'm riding—so I grabbed a bottle of orange juice from a machine at the track before I put a couple of horses through their morning workouts. The trainer cut the workouts short because the track was muddy from the overnight rain. That left me time to go out for a real breakfast."

"This trainer—could he or someone else have slipped something in the juice?"

"Not Nealon Donnelly. I've known him for years. He trains horses for Edgemoor Farms. If I hadn't smashed up on Bury My Heart, I would've been riding his horses later that day. Besides, I finished the juice before I even stepped in the barn."

"Bury My Heart wasn't his horse?"

"No. Chris Knight was riding the Edgemoor horse in that race."

"Do you get along with Nealon?"

"Sure. He's a big old bear, but a teddy bear, not a grizzly. The only thing that makes him mad is a jock who doesn't follow the game plan."

She grinned as she stretched my leg toward the ceiling and extended my hamstring a few inches farther than it wanted to go. "Do you always do as you're told?"

I groaned. "Where horses are concerned. I ride 'em like the trainer wants. That's my job."

"Did this Nealon Donnelly offer you anything to eat or drink?"

I shook my head, then said, "Wait! Chris Knight was there. And so was Luis Castenon, the other jock who rides for Edgemoor. Nealon wanted to talk to all of us together, so I hung around. He gave me a stick of chewing gum while we waited. It had a really strong licorice flavor. He orders it special because everybody used to chew it down South when he was a kid. I thought it was foul."

She raised her eyebrows and gave me a pointed look.

"But how could dope get in gum?" I asked.

"They used to put drops of LSD on sugar cubes. Why not on a stick of gum?"

I rubbed my forehead, trying to grasp the idea that someone wanted me dead or maimed. Nealon was certainly no enemy. I'd brought home a lot of wins for Edgemoor Farms. Not as many as Chris; he seemed to be on a permanent winning streak and was Edgemoor's fair-haired boy. But still, there was no bad blood between me and Nealon. Far from it.

"No," I finally said, "it couldn't have been Nealon."

"Okay. Tell me about breakfast. Who went?"

"Let's see. Nealon gave us his decision on Derby mounts and went off to some meeting of his own. So it was just me, the other two jocks, and my agent, Jimmy Dobbins. We went to Chick's Café. It's a little mom-and-pop diner a couple of blocks from the track. They start serving breakfast at 4:00 A.M. and do a mean egg-white omelet."

She made a face. "Yuck. Who wants an egg-white omelet?"

I decided to let Teri in on the facts of life, jockey style. "Lying in this bed has fattened me up. I've put on fifteen pounds. My usual weight is a hundred and eight. That means I get to eat about a thousand calories a day. Any more and I'm too heavy to ride."

"So you're on a perpetual diet?"

"It's either that or hit the flipping sink."

Her eyes questioned me as her firm hands massaged the wasted muscles of my bad leg.

"A lot of jockeys can't stay away from food," I explained. "They eat what they want and make weight by heaving it back up. Take Chris Knight, for instance. He's five-six. No way he can eat normally and keep his weight where it has to be. Every morning he weighs in to see what he needs to lose. Then he gets in the sweatbox and hits the sink until he's lost it."

"Sounds dangerous, Matt. A couple of girls I knew in high school had to be put in the hospital for that very thing. Do the track officials know about it?"

"Know about it? Who do you think installed the sweatbox and the special sink in the jockeys' locker room right between the showers and the toilets?" I sighed. "If we can't make weight, they don't have a horse race. The track doesn't make any money."

"I get the picture." She nodded thoughtfully. "The egg-white omelet—is that all you had for breakfast?"

"I had some coffee. Probably two cups, black."

"Who poured that coffee?"

"Chick's is just a hole-in-the-wall with a counter and six booths. We sat at the counter with the grill right in front of our noses. I saw the cook fry up my omelet and the counter guy pour my coffee."

"Did you eat anything else?"

"Well, I *usually* have one piece of dry toast to scoop up the omelet."

"Usually? But not that morning?"

I felt my cheeks growing red. "I had my toast, but then I totally lost it. The cook was warming some honey buns on the griddle.

I was so hungry, and they just smelled so good."

"You had one?"

"Worse than that. I had two."

The beeper clipped to Teri's waistband came to life with a raucous screech, and I jumped as far as a man tethered to a block and tackle can jump.

She gave the device a glance and said, "Looks like we're done for this morning, but I'm giving you an assignment. Before I come back for your afternoon session, I want you to figure out who would stand to gain if you'd broken your neck on that track."

I responded by running my hand down her arm to clasp her hand. "You're pretty good at this investigation stuff, lady. Are you sure you don't have a night job with the Metro Police?"

She grinned, letting my hand stay where it was. "I don't, but my dad does. He's been a homicide detective for twenty years. When I was a kid, he had us solving cases around the dinner table every night."

After Teri left, my room seemed darker and a hell of a lot lonelier. Lunch came, but I didn't eat much. When the lime-green Jell-O is the tastiest thing on the tray, you don't have much incentive. Then the nurse tried to get me to take a pain pill, but I didn't want that either. I had a lot of thinking to do, and I needed my brain up and running.

In my head, I traveled back to the breakfast counter at Chick's. Chris had taken the stool to my left. He'd downed a plate of biscuits and sausage gravy followed by a couple of those honey buns that I was craving. He was totally into feeding his face; I didn't recall that he even glanced at my plate. Jimmy sat on the other side of Chris. To sneak something into my food or coffee, the agent would have had to lean over Chris and really stretch. Or get up and come around Chris to me.

I squeezed my brain like a tube of toothpaste. No, I was sure that Jimmy hadn't left his stool until we'd all finished eating and were getting into our jackets. In fact, he'd seemed unusually quiet.

I thought it was because of Nealon's announcement. The trainer had tapped Chris to ride the Edgemoor favorite in the Derby and decided to put Luis on their field horse. I hadn't been surprised. Both those jocks rode exclusively for Edgemoor; I just filled in. But it meant Jimmy would have to get busy to find me a Derby mount.

Luis had sat on my right during breakfast. I don't know why I even bothered to consider him. Luis wouldn't put me in harm's way; he practically worshipped the ground I walked on. He'd shown up on the Southern racing circuit four or five years earlier, a skinny teenager just up from Mexico with only a few apprentice rides under his belt. He didn't look like much, but the kid had a good feel for horses, along with that all-important fire to win. I showed him the ropes and hooked him up with the right people, including the lawyer who'd helped him get his green card and bring his family up from their godforsaken village south of Mexico City.

Luis never forgot the favor. Once he started raking in some bucks, he bought a little bungalow in Louisville, and he had me over for dinner every time I rode at Churchill. His mother would stuff me with refritos and empanadas while an army of sisters and female cousins argued over who got to sit next to me on the couch. I envied Luis that home. Someday I planned to trade living out of a suitcase for a little house just like his, right down to the vines and flowers growing up the trellised front porch.

That was it. Thanks to the honey buns, I was seriously worried about making weight, so I didn't consume so much as another crumb before I went down to the paddock to mount Bury My Heart for the second race on that day's card.

When Teri came back, I was ready to throw in the towel. "I've racked my brain, but this whole thing makes no sense. None of the people I was around that morning had a reason to kill me."

She perched one hip on the side of my bed. "I've been think-ing, too. Maybe *you* weren't the target. Your horse, the one that had to be put down, was she a winner?"

"She was showing a lot of promise. Her owner planned to run her in the Oaks." I tried to recall the track buzz I'd heard about the entry slate for the Oaks, the filly race that was little sister to the Derby and carried a nice purse. "Bury My Heart was one of the two favorites, as a matter of fact."

"Okay. Was Nealon Donnelly planning to run a horse in the Oaks?"

I nodded enthusiastically. "Yeah, the other favorite *was* an Edgemoor Farms filly. Chris was riding her when I had my spill."

"There you go," she said triumphantly. "Nealon gave you spiked gum because you were riding Bury My Heart. He wanted that horse injured or dead so *his* filly wouldn't have any competi-tion in the Oaks."

"It won't work, Teri," I answered after a moment's thought. "There are so many variables out on the track—a race can go a hundred different ways. Bury My Heart could have easily gone down and taken the Edgemoor horse out with her. Nealon would never have risked it. No true horseman would."

I stared at my bandaged leg glumly. "I've just got to face it. I'll never be able to prove I wasn't on dope and get my jockey's license back. You've been giving me all these exercises for nothing—a big, fat bunch of nothing."

Teri crossed her arms and drilled me with determined green eyes. "If this is how easily you quit, Matt LeMaster, I'm surprised you ever won any races."

I grimaced. "I have to face facts."

"The only important fact is that someone slipped you a hallu-cinogenic drug, and we have to figure out who. Now think! What about that agent who went to breakfast with you?"

"Don't pick on Jimmy. Agents don't make any money unless

their jocks do. Jimmy takes a twenty-five-percent commission on all my fees and winnings. The last thing he'd want is to have me sidelined."

"Not if he was hiding something from you. A little fiddling with the accounts, maybe?"

I didn't answer. Something Jimmy had been complaining about started needling the back of my brain.

"Well?" Teri asked. "Does Jimmy have money problems?"

"I don't know," I answered slowly, not liking the suspicion that was dawning. "But his son-in-law does. That guy's been ditching work to spend time at the OTB and the gambling boat. Jimmy told me his daughter had to cancel their credit cards and take a second job."

"Could Jimmy have been skimming some of your pay to help his daughter out of a jam? And been afraid what you'd do when you found out?"

I shrugged. "I *had* asked to see a copy of the tax returns he filed for me. Not that I suspected anything, just as a check."

The therapist rolled her eyes. "Why didn't you just paint a big bull's-eye on your chest?"

"Aw, Teri, don't say that. Jimmy's a pal. Besides, he didn't have any opportunity to mess with my food."

Teri dropped the Jimmy theory, but she wouldn't let me rest. Sure that I was forgetting something important, she kept up a barrage of questions while she worked my muscles. Her enthusiasm gradually conquered my black mood. I related everything I'd considered during the afternoon, including my longing for a vine-covered cottage. But I still couldn't think of anything else that had passed my lips. Not on the way in.

I was ashamed to admit it, but when I finally confessed that I'd had to hit the flipping sink to make weight, Teri had a brainwave. "Did you wash your mouth out after you vomited?"

"Yeah, sure. I took my water bottle in with me, but I only swallowed a few sips. I mainly swished the water around my mouth to get rid of the bad taste, then spit it out. No sense adding another ounce when you've got two pounds to get rid of."

"Was anyone else around?"

I thought for a minute. "Chris Knight was ahead of me. He'd already put his water bottle on the shelf over the sink, but he told me to go on. He likes to wait till the last minute before weigh-in."

Teri's eyes were sparkling. She dug her hands into my thigh muscle and squeezed. "Think, Matt. Was anyone else there?"

"Ouch, that's my bad leg. Remember?"

"Who else? There had to be someone."

"There were a lot of guys in the locker room—jockeys, their valets, the clerk of scales, the track chaplain."

"But right there at the sink, within arm's length."

"The water was running in the shower stall behind the sink, but I don't know who was in there."

Teri whooped and threw her arms up like a wide receiver catching a pass in the end zone. "I do, Matt. I know!"

The next few days were an exercise in patience—not my strong suit. Teri wouldn't tell me who she figured for my would-be murderer. "It's in Dad's hands now," she said. "I explained my theory, and he's got the crime lab working on it. After the tests come back, we'll know if I'm right or wrong. Then I'll spill everything."

Each time I pressed her, she'd say, "Not yet, not till I'm certain," then turn the conversation to other things. Lots of other things.

On a sunny day in mid-June, I was tracking fluffy clouds from a chair by the window, aching to be flying around a track on a fresh Thoroughbred. My mangled leg had healed enough to be released from its harness, allowing me to put some weight on it. The doctor said that with a little luck, I might get back to riding by the end of the year. I could hardly wait, but riding didn't mean making a living. For that, I'd need a reprieve from the Racing Commission. So far I had nothing that was likely to change their minds about my suspension.

The door clicked, and I looked up to see Teri, followed by a short, stocky man in a rumpled suit. He had a brush of graying red hair and green eyes that matched hers.

"Frank O'Callahan, Metro Police," he said as he extended a hand. "We've got some good news for you, Matt."

"You know who slipped me the Mickey?"

He nodded his protruding jaw and said, "I'll let Teri tell it."

Tease that she was, Teri kept beating around the bush, spinning out the suspense until I threatened to hobble over and beat her over the head with my crutch.

"Stay put, Matt. I've put in too much work on that tibia to risk it." She laughed, then got down to business. "I kept thinking about those old Aztec witch doctors drinking their hallucinogenic tea. What if someone took a similar tea and distilled it—condensed it until only a few drops could send you straight to the stratosphere? Then you mentioned someone who might have access to flowers like the Aztecs used."

I shook my head, mystified. "I know a lot of people, but none of them are ancient Aztecs."

She lowered herself onto a stool by my chair. Solemn now, she said, "But you do know someone from southern Mexico. I checked a history book; that's the region the Aztecs ruled. Their traditions are still part of the culture, especially in rural areas."

"Luis," I whispered. "Luis and his bungalow covered with flowering vines." I pictured the Mexican jock—my good friend, I'd thought—for a long moment of anguish. "But why? Why would he want to kill me?"

"It wasn't supposed to be you," Teri answered quickly. "Luis was trying to get Chris Knight out of the way so Nealon Donnelly would put him on Edgemoor's Derby favorite. Dead or discredited—it really didn't matter, as long as Chris wasn't riding. Luis had one of those plastic water bottles that everybody uses laced with the drug. He took it into the shower with him, knowing that Chris always flipped before he weighed in. But then you showed up. Luis ended up exchanging water bottles with you instead of Chris."

"If it's any comfort," Detective O'Callahan added in a gravelly bass, "the kid was sick about it, eaten up with guilt. As soon as we confronted him with the toxicology report on the flowers growing up his porch, he broke down and confessed the whole plan. His mother raised those flowers from seeds she'd brought from her village. She brewed them up according to an age-old recipe. It was the old lady who nagged him into dosing that other jock. She didn't think her Luis was getting his fair share of mounts. She was determined to give him a shot at winning the Derby."

"I guess the jock's share of the million-dollar Derby purse was just an added inducement," I said.

The detective nodded. "You don't support a houseful of relatives plus family back in Mexico by riding field horses. Luis needed some serious cash—he saw a chance to bring home a Derby win and break into the ranks of the top moneymakers."

One of my hands found Teri's; I extended the other to her father. "I can't thank you enough, Detective O'Callahan. If it weren't for you and Teri, my career would be history."

He grinned as he shook my hand. "Better call me Frank, son. My daughter tells me we're going to be seeing a lot of each other."

For some, the long shot in a race is the horse that doesn't have much of a chance of winning. Still, stranger things have happened. The odds on a horse, or what the bettors perceive to be the horse's chance of winning, determine whether the horse is considered a long shot. The higher the number, the longer the odds.

The last long shot to win the Kentucky Derby was Ferdinand in 1986; the odds were 17-1. The best payoff came in 1913, when Donerail had the longest winning odds, 91.45 to 1, paying close to $185 for every $2 bet. Now, that was a winning ticket.

In horse racing, the bettors bet against each other, not against the horse. This system, devised in France, is called "pari-mutuel." If the bettor thinks his pick will "win," he purchases that ticket. In order to cash in the ticket, the horse *must* win. A bet to "place" means the horse comes in first or second in order to cash the ticket. The safe bet, to "show," gives the bettor three opportunities to win some money: the horse has to come in first, second, or third to collect. Many combinations of the three basic bets can pay off large or wipe you out all at once.

THE LONG SHOT
by P. J. Robertson

———✠———

P. J. Robertson has degrees in psychology, history, and education, as well as extensive graduate work in sociology. After teaching sociology for several years at a Midwestern university, she returned to her first love, the mystery novel. She is now editing her first completed book. She lives in Southern Indiana with her husband, where she trains and shows Bouvier des Flandres dogs.

SUEANN HURST'S VIEW through her kitchen window wavered as if reflected in an antique looking glass. She noted the few surviving flowers that thrust their sturdy stems through the cracked clay soil next door, part of the young couple's feeble attempt to spruce up the aging trailer on its tiny lot. The fresh paint they'd brushed over the rusting hulk only served to remind SueAnn of her own futile pretense that things were better than they actually were. She gently touched the windowpane. Let them hang on to their dreams.

Tearing a paper towel from the roll, she swiped at the tears coursing down her cheeks. Some people might call these manufactured houses, or even mobile homes, but looking around her own minuscule kitchen and living room, she knew there was no sense pretending—these were nothing but trailers, metal shells lined with cheap paneling, outdated carpeting, and shabby furniture. And to call this a trailer park, why that was clearly a misnomer; there was nothing park-like about this setting.

I grew up in a trailer park, she thought. *I thought I'd escaped, but here I am again.* She sighed, blowing her nose on the paper towel before tossing it into the trash can under the sink. *Bobby may be ready to give up on life, but I'm not; I haven't lived yet.* She raised her chin and straightened her shoulders. *I'm not usually such a crybaby; it must be these darn onions.*

Ignoring the tears that threatened to fill her eyes again, SueAnn scraped the coarsely chopped onions into a glass bowl, atop the minced garlic, and began disemboweling the large red tomatoes lined up on the pitted countertop. She used a serrated knife to cut off thick slices, then grabbed the sharp chef's knife to chop them into large chunks.

Bobby loved her salsa, but he wanted his vegetables in big pieces. She cut the jalapeños in half and threw them in the bowl. This time she'd added some new varieties the Food Lion store advertised as being even hotter than jalapeños. The fiery little habanero peppers were chopped fine. She washed her hands carefully after chopping those, her skin burning from the juices.

Spices were added last. She scooped over half the mixture into the food processor for a quick whir. No one but Bobby liked the big chunks, and today she'd give it to him just like he wanted, but his buddies would appreciate the finer version.

She'd refused to make the salsa since Bobby had developed trouble with his throat. He'd nearly choked the last time she'd fixed it, but he'd refused to see a doctor. To be honest, there was no money for a doctor; her salary and tips went only so far, after all. Besides, no one could talk Bobby into doing anything he didn't want to—all his friends knew that. And he didn't choke often, just when he was excited.

Covering both bowls with plastic wrap, she set the salsa in the refrigerator to chill.

Bobby had asked for her salsa, special, for this party. It was Derby day, and he'd invited a few of his cronies over to watch the big race. They got together for every big sporting event to eat, drink, and bet on the outcome. She wasn't sure any of them cared about the race, or knew its history. She wasn't sure they even considered it a sport at all, but it was an excuse to get together and do what they did best.

So she'd made his favorite salsa, just like he preferred it, and today, well, today maybe she just didn't care if Bobby choked. She would put out both bowls, and he could make his choice.

She checked the beer supply. Bobby had been furious when she'd brought home generic beer, but she'd stuck to her guns, for once. Generic beer or no beer—and since she bought the groceries, he'd had no choice but to agree. Sometimes she felt guilty when she remembered the few precious pieces of antique pewter she had wrapped in old towels and secreted in the trunk of her car. She had few treasures, heaven only knew, but Bobby would be quick to sell the pewter if he knew it existed and had value. *Sell it to buy more beer or make more bets,* she thought unkindly.

Standing on the worn vinyl tile in front of the window, she gazed around the small living room and even tinier kitchen, divided only by a counter and the back of their sofa. She wrinkled her nose. She'd cleaned, but the sofa's brown-and-tan upholstery fabric sported some type of pheasant or grouse hiding in bushes, the birds barely discernible beneath the decades-old grime. And no matter how she scrubbed, it never looked clean.

A large-screen television, Bobby's pride and joy, blocked the light from the trailer's front window. Their last tax refund had paid for the television. Was it her imagination, or did the blank screen seem to suck light from the room? Bobby's bowling trophies filled the glass shelves hung across the side windows, just as his old high school football trophies cluttered the spare bedroom.

No place in the cramped trailer was really hers. She dreamed of a sparsely furnished Cape Cod cottage, with a few of her pewter pieces displayed on its tastefully painted mantel. Sometimes in her daydreams the mantel was painted an historic blue hue; other times it glowed a rich mustard in the dappled light streaming through the blown-glass windowpanes.

She shook the cobwebs from her head. Like she would achieve that dream, working as she did at the truck stop just across the state line, and with Bobby losing his license as well as being fired from the trucking company after that last accident. She'd thought he'd known better than to drink when he had a load to deliver.

She had to hide her tip money, or Bobby would demand it too. She wished she had the strength to resist him, but she'd felt so tired, so worn, since the death of their infant son, Cody. The memory of that pale, limp form, drawing its first and last breath within the same short hour, haunted her. Some genetic illness, according to her doctor; she'd been too distraught to understand or remember exactly what. On the advice of her doctor and her husband, she'd had her tubes tied. That hurt more, perhaps, than little Cody's death, because her dream had died as well. Any chance for the family she'd always wanted had vanished. She'd thought Bobby was as devastated as she was by thoughts of their childless future, but sometimes she wondered if he could really care as much, hurt as much, as she.

She remembered their first years together, the way Bobby depended on her. She was the strong one. She'd helped him with his homework, written his research papers, tutored him before his tests, and stroked his ego when he realized he was no longer the big man on campus he'd been in high school. Despite her help, he lost his football scholarship. He was crushed, so lost. She'd cradled his head against her breasts while he cried. It was then he asked her to be his bride.

He needed her and so she married him. She fought to finish her education even after she became pregnant, but her ambition had died along with her son. She gave up the academic scholarship her mother was so proud of. With Bobby working one low-paying job after another, the first few years had been tough and they'd needed her income. She went back to the only job she'd ever known, the job she'd done every summer since she was old enough to carry a loaded tray. From childhood, she'd done her homework seated in a restaurant booth while her mother worked, so it seemed waitressing ran in her blood.

By the time Bobby found a job driving the big trucks and could support them, she didn't want to quit. She liked having her own money, to spend on whatever things they couldn't afford on his income.

Only last fall had she realized she wanted to do more, and she signed up for a couple of classes to ease back into her degree program. She loved history. She didn't know how it would help her earn a living, but she decided to major in it anyway. A good thing she'd held onto her job, though, 'cause Bobby had the wreck just after Christmas, and now her income was all they had. Goodbye to classes; she had to work all the hours she could get.

Sure, Bobby had needed a few weeks for the bones to mend, but it seemed his mind was more broken yet. He refused to look for work, sitting in the trailer all day, watching television and drinking generic beer. Polishing those damned trophies.

The television screen was dark now. As soon as Bobby came in, it would spew color and noise until he fell asleep, sprawled drunkenly on the sofa. Only then could she turn it off.

She heard bare feet slap the vinyl floor. Bobby must be out of bed. She popped the top on a can of beer. He would want one first thing; he claimed it helped with his hangover from the night before.

The night before. SueAnn had tried to forget about last night. She busied herself hauling bags of chips out of the cabinets overhead, pouring the chips into bowls. Luckily, Bobby didn't mind generic chips. He evidently wasn't too fussy about what he ate or drank, going by the gut hanging over the towel twisted around his once-trim waist. As predicted, he turned the can upside down and chugged the beer, leaving the empty can for her to dispose of. His red-rimmed eyes refused to meet hers as he grabbed another beer and went back down the hall. SueAnn heard the shower start.

It had been a big mistake, forgetting about the lottery ticket. She'd been so surprised when the old man left her a $20 tip, just for taking a little extra time to chat with him about his wife. Losing her still hurt him so much—even after more than two years, she could tell—and it wasn't real busy when he'd been in. She'd stopped at the store to buy Bobby's lottery tickets, the same way she did every Friday on her way home. Tennessee didn't allow gambling, so she and Bobby did what many Tennessee residents did—played Kentucky's lottery. She'd gotten the strangest urge to buy a ticket of her own, and so she'd asked for her special numbers. Then she'd stuck the slip of paper into her wallet, along with Bobby's tickets, and forgotten it.

And last night, when the numbers were being drawn, Bobby had searched her wallet for his tickets, and grabbed hers as well. After all the years of buying tickets, and all the losing tickets thrown in the trash, wouldn't you know *her* ticket would bear the winning numbers. Bobby was dumbstruck, but he held the ticket high above her head and crowed about what he'd won. He was already planning how he would spend the money. And SueAnn saw her dreams vanishing once more.

"All those numbers I've chosen so carefully," he'd said, "and you walk in and pick out any old numbers and win."

That had hurt as much as anything he'd ever said to her. He didn't recognize the numbers—the birth date of their only child, their dead child. As if *she* could forget.

They'd argued, she knew, but she'd banished the words from her mind so she could go on. And once he'd fallen asleep on the sofa, she'd searched for the ticket. It wasn't in his wallet, nor was it beneath the stained underwear in his drawer, nor any of the secret places where women put things they want to keep hidden. Expanding her search, she found it where he'd tucked it, beneath his biggest football trophy: the monument to all he had once been or had ever wanted to be. Now the precious wisp of paper was hidden away in a safe place, a place she knew he'd never think to look. SueAnn wrapped her arms tightly around her body; Bobby would be in a rage when he discovered it missing.

He came into the living room, dressed in his usual jeans and tee. He'd no more than activated the television when his three cronies appeared, as though brought into existence by the push of a button on the remote control. Beers were handed round, and they settled in to watch the pre-race show and select their sure bets.

"Last time we'll have to drink generic beer, boys," Bobby said, with a quick glance at his wife.

The men, already engrossed in the show, didn't respond.

SueAnn made sure all the dishes were full of chips and dip. She set the two bowls of salsa near the tortilla chips and removed the plastic, pushed the stack of plates an inch closer to the bowls. The men filed into the small space awkwardly and filled their plates with chips and dip, grabbing beers she'd set out for them.

She wondered if any of them realized they were about to watch the oldest sporting event in the United States. Ironically, she'd learned that fact while watching America's second oldest sporting event, the Westminster Dog Show. She hadn't known such a thing existed until late one winter evening, she'd channel-surfed past a ring full of dogs of all descriptions, and stopped, riveted. That was when Bobby still drove a truck and overnight runs out of town were frequent. This past February, with Bobby out of a job, she'd retired early so she could watch the dogs parade silently across the small television screen suspended opposite their double bed.

Bobby wouldn't even agree to her having a pet. "I won't have some useless, wimpy little dog," he'd said. "We can't afford to feed one anyway. If we had money for a *real* dog, it'd be different."

SueAnn had known just what kind of dog he envisioned, the kind he and his friends referred to as *rockwallers,* a name that scraped across her nerves like fingernails across a blackboard. She hadn't bothered to correct him, just as she hadn't invited him to watch the dog show with her. For Bobby, a sporting event meant gambling, and she shuddered as she imagined him and his friends betting on the group winners as well as Best in Show. No, she'd watched, and dreamed, alone.

The once-tidy living room began to reek of beer. Chips already littered the shag carpeting she'd vacuumed that morning, and cigarette ashes powdered the end tables. Bobby might not clean house, but it didn't take long for him and his friends to dirty it. She started toward the bedroom, anxious to retreat from the smoke fumes, but when the announcers introduced the colts running in the race, she paused, fascinated by the muscular horses.

Bobby picked up the phone. "Y'all ready to place your bets?" He punched in the number so familiar to him—that of his local bookie. "Okay, here we go. I'm feeling lucky today." He grinned up at his wife. "Next year we'll watch the race from one of those boxes at the track, boys."

He couldn't wait to brag about *his* lottery win, she knew. She'd begged him to wait, let them actually claim the money before he told his friends. Finally, he'd agreed, but he couldn't help giving small hints.

One by one, Bobby and his friends placed their bets. As Bobby was about to hang up, SueAnn made her decision and took the receiver from his hand.

"I want to place a bet."

He stared at her, openmouthed.

"Yes, this is Bobby's wife, SueAnn. I want to bet a thousand dollars on the one who just went by, number twelve. Yes, the long shot, fifty to one. That's right. Thanks." She handed him the phone.

The guys hooted.

"Why did you pick that nag?" Bobby wanted to know. "He doesn't stand a chance. How are you going to pay for that bet, anyway?"

SueAnn stubbornly refused to back down. "He has an intelligent face. And I think he will win. It doesn't hurt to bet on long shots once in while; sometimes they pay off." She walked off down the hall to their bedroom, closing the door firmly behind her, not that the flimsy rectangle would keep out much noise.

She turned on the small television; it was time for her favorite antiques show. Mrs. Stroud, the trailer park's ancient owner, had graciously been educating her and helping her add to her pewter collection. The old lady was secretive about her treasures, and SueAnn felt honored that Mrs. Stroud trusted her. And Mrs. Stroud had recommended the show, so SueAnn watched it religiously. She turned up the sound so she could hear over the shouts from the men.

A loud "Yeah!" came from the other room. She assumed the horse race had begun.

Unfortunately for her husband, a pewter tea set was the focus of the two antiques show hosts, so it was several seconds before SueAnn realized the sounds from the living room were not the usual cheers and jeers of sports fans. And her name was being called. Screamed, really.

She hurriedly rose and opened the door. She could hear Bobby's choking from there, and the yells as his drunken friends tried to help.

She ran down the hall, shrieking her husband's name. He was still seated on the sofa where she'd left him, but now his body was arched as he tried to draw breath, without success. His eyes bulged out of a face turned blue, pleading with her to do something. One friend pulled him forward, pounded on his back, trying to dislodge the piece of food now blocking Bobby's windpipe.

Tomato or onion? SueAnn wondered. *Or maybe the pepper?*

She pulled Chet away from her husband. "Sean, you have the longest fingers. You try to get the food out of there while I call for an ambulance." She began to search for the cordless phone, last seen in Bobby's hand. "Where's the phone?" She dropped to her knees and ran her hand along the carpet, underneath the skirted sofa. She rose, empty-handed.

"I'll run over to Mrs. Stroud's to call." She avoided looking at Bobby, at his beseeching eyes.

SueAnn stumbled as one of the concrete blocks that made up their trailer's steps rocked under her feet. She landed awkwardly, twisting her ankle. *Damn Bobby,* she thought, *I've asked him over and over to do something about that block.*

She limped as fast as she could across the neighbors' yards to Mrs. Stroud's door. "Please, Mrs. Stroud, it's an emergency. I need to use your phone!"

The door opened and thin arms pulled her inside. Within minutes, she'd called 911 and given directions to her home. As she limped back toward the trailer with the old woman beside her, sirens swooped near. A white emergency vehicle slid to a stop beside her old Chevette, and two men in dark uniforms raced into the trailer, carrying their equipment with them. Mrs. Stroud's stringy arms held her back. SueAnn sagged in her hold.

In a few minutes, the medics returned, unloaded a stretcher, and whisked it up the steps into the trailer's cramped living room. SueAnn could stand it no longer. She wrenched herself loose and ran for the trailer, her limp forgotten. As she reached the trailer door, it opened. Chet, Bobby's best friend, held the door for the medics as they carried the loaded stretcher out to the ambulance. Suddenly sober, Chet looked at SueAnn and shook his head. He put his arms around her. "I'm so sorry, SueAnn. Nothing we did seemed to help."

The older medic approached. "We're sorry, we were just too late. The doctor will have to declare him dead, but he's gone." He took her hand. "When you make arrangements, tell the funeral director he can call the hospital in a couple of hours about pickup." He dropped her hand and touched his fingers to his cap, then returned to the vehicle. It pulled away, siren silent, the sound of its engine fading away quickly.

Bobby's friends quietly filed out of the trailer. Chet offered to stay, but SueAnn, dry-eyed, asked to be alone. He pulled her close, and SueAnn stiffened when his hand casually brushed against her breast as he released her. "Just let me know how I can help," he said. Then they were gone.

Assured that she wasn't needed, Mrs. Stroud reluctantly left. SueAnn entered the deserted trailer, alone. She stood, looking around at the furniture pushed from its normal arrangement, the crushed chips, and overturned bowls of dip and salsa. The television blared on, some commercial extolling the virtues of a special toothpaste. Locating the remote, she switched it off. Then, collecting some garbage bags and rubber gloves from beneath the sink, she began to clean. And as she cleaned, she began to hum.

She emptied the bowls of their remaining contents and scrubbed the worn carpet, pulling and pushing the furniture back into place. She was glad no one was there to see as she collected boxes from the shed and began to empty the shelves of their heavy burden. Bobby's trophies soon filled the boxes, which were then carefully carried one by one to the end of the drive and stacked for garbage pickup. Choosing one more box, she emptied the refrigerator of its beer and added that to the pile.

When the room was tidied and emptied of all signs of Bobby, as though finishing the task brought on the action, the telephone rang. SueAnn scooped the phone from beneath the sofa, where her searching fingers had lightly brushed against its hard plastic casing such a short time before.

"Hello," she answered, her voice hoarse.

"SueAnn, Chet stopped by the restaurant to tell me about Bobby." Her best friend's voice sounded so loud coming over the phone line, into the silent living room. "Should I come over? You shouldn't be alone."

"No, Becca. I really want to be alone. You're a good friend to want to come, but I know you need to work your shift, and really, I'm okay. It's just all so sad, somehow. Did you know we'd won some money on the lottery? Not a fortune, but enough to get us out of debt. We had so many plans, Becca." Tears ran down SueAnn's cheeks. She sobbed quietly, but still loud enough for her friend to hear.

"Oh, SueAnn. I am so sorry. Just tell me how I can help, please."

SueAnn assured her friend she would tell her when she needed help. She hesitated, and then asked, "Becca, did you hear who won the race? With Bobby choking and all, no one was watching. . . ."

"Oh, SueAnn!" Becca was now openly weeping. "It's scary. Chet mentioned your bet. I've never known you to do such a thing! And the horse. . . ."

"What do you mean? Tell me," she pleaded.

"It was that horse you bet on, the long shot. It won! What was its name? Something foreign?"

SueAnn smiled. "The long shot? Really, he won? That was a horse named Heimlich Maneuver. . . ." She quickly said good-bye to her friend, turned off the phone, and returned it to its base. She looked around the room, clean once again, picked up a couple more boxes, and headed down the hall to the spare bedroom. A few football trophies to go, plus Bobby's clothes, and she would be finished.

Their argument from the night before was now clear in her

mind. And she remembered exactly when she decided leaving Bobby wasn't enough, that he had to die.

You're fixated on that baby, SueAnn. You've become an old lady. We'll take the money and have us some fun. C'mon, don't you want to have fun?

Adopt a baby? I don't think so. We don't need kids; we've got each other. Aren't you glad I insisted you have your tubes tied? It's been hard enough for you to recover from Cody's death. You could have had three or four like that before you had one that lived, normal-like, just like my Aunt Paula did. Nearly broke her heart each time, it did.

What? So I didn't tell you the problem came from my side of the family. What difference does it make? We're together, a team. Bobby had laughed. *After all, you weren't going to have a baby without me, now, were you?*

By the spring of 1943, with the United States in the middle of World War II, the government had ordered restrictions on travel. Matt Winn, president of Churchill Downs, wrote to all non-Louisville boxholders and asked them to purchase tickets but not attend. Limitations were placed on automobiles within a mile of the racetrack, prompting the 69th Run for the Roses to be dubbed the Streetcar Derby. Only 62,000 locals saw Count Fleet begin his sweep of the Triple Crown.

As America sent more men to fight, the Office of Defense Transportation placed a ban on horse races and requested that Winn put a stop to racing at Churchill Downs. Winn countered with a suggestion that tickets from the boxholders could be turned over to military personnel. From that point on, uniforms dominated the racetrack.

The Kentucky Derby almost lost its streak of consecutive years when the government issued a final ban on horse racing in 1945. But VE Day brought an end to the ban, and the race was run on June 9 that year.

THE CASE OF THE DERBY DIAMOND

by Jeffrey Marks

Jeffrey Marks was born in Georgetown, Ohio, the boyhood home of Ulysses S. Grant. Although he moved with his family at an early age, the family frequently told stories about Grant and the people of the small farming community. After writing numerous author profiles, he chose to chronicle the short but full life of mystery writer Craig Rice. That biography (which came out in April 2001 as Who Was That Lady?*) encouraged him to write mystery fiction. His work has won a number of awards including the Barnes and Noble Prize, and he was nominated for an Edgar (MWA), an Agatha (Malice Domestic), a Maxwell (DWAA), and an Anthony (Bouchercon). Today, he writes from his home in Cincinnati, which he shares with his partner, their ward, and a Scottish terrier.*

I DIDN'T SEE HOW Mrs. Van Hoskin could tell that she was missing a particular necklace. She had more ice than the Titanic. Of course, the rich use both hands to grasp everything that they own. Still, the Derby Diamond had quite a colorful history. The dame's grandfather had commissioned the necklace—a jewel-encrusted horseshoe surrounding a seven-carat diamond—to commemorate one of the earliest horse races in Louisville, nearly seventy years earlier. The current owner, married to one of the town's leading industrialists, wore the diamond only once a year on the occasion of her annual Derby party. Rumor had it that it took two sets of hands to hang it on a woman's neck and fix the clasp.

Me, I was lucky to be able to have one hand to hold anything in. I'd lost my right hand at Okinawa and been shipped home to Louisville. I couldn't go back to my job as a cop; no one wants a right-handed man aiming a gun with his left. So I got my PI license and waited around for a way to make some dough. The war had made it tough on everyone, but the rich still lounged at home while others fought for freedom.

One of my friends on the force had tossed me this case. The upper crust didn't want a fuss made about the loss of the jewels; Mr. Van H had informed me over the phone that he just wanted it back without a hubbub.

That's the way it worked when it was one of your own. Besides, the scuttlebutt was that the diamonds hadn't made her faithful. She'd been rumored to be stepping out on her husband.

So I'd come to the Van Hoskin home to talk to the dame about her missing necklace. I figured she suspected someone in particular of taking it. If the maid had stolen it, she would have wanted the full treatment from the force. That left her high-class friends. No one in Glenview would be subjected to the third degree. It was all velvet gloves and polite questions off River Road.

Mrs. Van Hoskin greeted me at the door. I'd been admiring the view from the bluffs. The Ohio River drifted idly by, oblivious to pain, suffering, and war. A guy could forget about Hirohito, looking at a river that had flowed for thousands of years.

None of the servants seemed to be around. Maybe they'd been shipped out to Pearl Harbor or beyond, like so many others. Or she didn't want the servants to know a thing about it.

"Won't you sit down, Mr. Donnelly?" She waved a hand at the knobby little chair in the entryway. It didn't look like something I'd want to sit in, but I did anyway. I was good enough to find her jewels, but not to be treated like a proper guest in the home.

"Thank you." I took a closer look around the room. The parlor was filled with stuff that looked like she'd taken it from a museum. I didn't see this kind of décor often. After all, I was from the West End, the other side of the world from Glenview. We didn't even visit the museums over there. There was no sign of Mr. Van Hoskin. Apparently, he spent a great deal of time away from home. There didn't seem to be much of his personality in what I could see of the house.

"When did you discover your necklace missing?" I asked, trying not to calculate my fee as we sat there.

"Well, as you may know, the Van Hoskins throw a Derby party every year. It's quite the event to attend." She made the announcement as if a spud like me might know it. "I wore it that evening and noticed it stolen at the end of the night."

"Someone heisted it off your neck?" I had a hard time seeing how that monstrosity would not be missed by even the richest of dames.

"No, I was wearing the diamond at the party, and the clasp broke. It fell down my décolletage, and I had to retrieve it."

She had the good graces to blush when she pronounced that word. I'd never heard it used in a sentence in my life. Real dames had bosoms. I knew then that I was way out of my league with this case. She played with the skin just under her three chins as if she wanted me to look just below them. I hadn't been with a woman since my wife had left, and I wasn't looking to change that with this dame. The cuckolded husband owned enough business in Jefferson County to make sure I'd never find work again.

"So you put it back on or stowed it aways somewhere?"

She wasn't the only one who could use words that the other wasn't likely to say.

"Well, I put it in my room until I could have a proper look at it. I couldn't abandon my guests that way." She gave me a look that could have wilted the Japs. Roosevelt could have used that expression for a secret weapon to win the war. "After all, one does not leave the Binghams waiting."

I bit my lip to suppress a smile. "No, of course not." Louisville's first family wanted nothing from me, so I figured I was safe in not caring.

"Well, the party was starting to break up anyway, so it wasn't a concern. After the last person left, I went back upstairs to see what had happened to the clasp, and the Derby Diamond was gone." Mrs. Van Hoskin had begun to pace the marble floor. Obviously the incident had upset her. Who could entertain when the guests were after your jewels and not your banter?

"Do you know who saw the necklace come off? How many people were around you?"

I could begin to see her worry. If she'd had the rock on all night, there wouldn't have been a chance to take it off her. The whole thing was a coincidence. Only the people who were still at the party after the clasp broke had the opportunity to heist it. The staff would have been too busy. Mrs. Van Hoskin didn't look like the type to let the help lounge around on her dime.

"I have the guest list. I've taken the liberty of marking off the names of the people who left early or weren't able to make it. In that way, you can see that there are only a few who would need to be bothered with an inquiry. I would expect your cooperation in keeping this on the QT."

"Of course." In all my years of police work, I'd never met an upper crust who didn't expect the entire investigation to be under wraps. The rich didn't do things any different than the rest of us; they just paid good money to keep it out of the papers. "I will have to ask a few questions of the people who were at the party. Other than that, no one needs to know."

I knew how true those words were. My life was four walls and a hot plate these days. My wife had left me when I'd come home unable to wrap my arms around her, and my office was a one-man business. Necessity to turn a buck, rather than liking to keep things lean and mean.

I decided to start with Miranda Beck, the well-known socialite. I knew that she wouldn't have had anything to do with the theft, but the thought of being in the same room with her was a tad intoxicating. I had seen her picture in the *Courier-Journal* since I'd been home. She was the kind of dame that I could get my arm around and not let go, but that wasn't likely to happen. Still she agreed to see me at the English Grill restaurant at the Brown Hotel for a drink. I wasn't up to buying dinner, but the drink seemed harmless enough. The lobby was full of boys stationed at Fort Knox, on leave for the weekend and seeing how the better half lived.

Miranda was sitting at a table when I arrived. Even with the shortage of hotel staff, she hadn't had a problem getting a drink. I doubted that she ever did. She tipped a martini and smiled at me. "So, how can I help with this? Are you really a private investigator? I've never met one before." She smiled again at me over the lip of the glass and made me forget why I'd come to the Brown.

Part of me wanted to hold her and forget the world for a while, but Mrs. Van Hoskin wouldn't appreciate that. Her rocks were the reason I was supposed to be here. I kept reminding myself of that as I tried not to stare at Miranda's beauty. She had the long neck of a swan and its graceful ease. Her blonde hair stroked her chiffon-covered shoulders and went well with the soft green of her gown and eyes. I would have gladly given both hands to keep her safe from the evil of the world.

I was surprised that she still ran with the swells, but I guess that tastes don't change as fast as circumstances. Her father had died in the stock market crash of 1929. He'd taken a long leap from a short building downtown when all of his clients' funds disappeared. He'd been playing fast and loose with other people's money.

Miranda had managed to land a good-looking member of society, but Herr Rommel had seen to his demise. Beck had been lost in North Africa, and he hadn't been heard of since then. Miranda still made the rounds of the social events, and the Derby was the event to end all events. Anyone who could muster a fancy gown would want to attend the Van Hoskins' party.

As it turned out, Miranda wasn't able to help me much with the case. She remembered the incident with the necklace and remembered Mrs. Van H putting it in her room, but that was about it. Mrs. Van Hoskin had fussed over the clasp, loud enough for everyone in the room to hear. Miranda mentioned a few people who had been in the room, but no one that my client hadn't highlighted for me. She scrunched up her face when one particular name came up in the conversation. I took that as a sign that perhaps the person in question didn't measure up to the social standards set by the elite of Louisville. Or it might have just been a bad smell in the air. But since I didn't have any other leads, I thought I might as well follow up on her unspoken ideas.

Miranda had turned up her nose at the name Mark Anderson, and I went to see him next. He was one of the few that I'd heard of on the guest list, and not in a good way. He had been linked to a number of married women throughout the first two years of the war. I wondered if Mrs. Van Hoskin was one of those women.

My ma cleaned for a few of the fancy folk up on the Glenview bluffs, and she'd heard stories. Once, she'd even seen Anderson leaving the home of a young war bride, well into the morning. Ma had gone on about that for three days.

I hadn't heard any mention of him before Pearl Harbor. He seemed to materialize out of thin air at the start of the war, to pick up the pieces for all the war widows and women who had been left alone during the early days of the fighting.

For some reason, despite his well-formed physique, he'd managed to come up 4-F with the draft board. It made me all the more suspicious of him. He hadn't appealed the ruling, and he'd stayed home while me and my buddies had gone off to fight the Japs.

My suspicions ended at the door. Anderson wasn't going to be telling me much of anything. In the past twelve hours or so, someone had taken a chunk out of his skull with a fireplace poker. The iron utensil still lay on the floor next to the body. He looked as if he'd been taken by surprise. His eyes were wide open, and his mouth formed a small O. The blood had sprayed across the room in an arc, telling me that whoever did this didn't hesitate to think twice about it.

I didn't touch a thing before calling my buddies on the force. I could hear them now, cussing me out for stumbling on more work for them. I was supposed to be taking the easy cases so they could stop in at Heitzman's Bakery for a doughnut or two.

I tried to take in the scene before they showed up, but I didn't see anything out of place or anything that looked like a tony necklace. I decided to help them out by tossing his bedroom before the boys showed up, but nothing was there to give me a hint on what had happened to the Derby Diamond.

Malloy stepped into the room and gave a long whistle. "You know how to pick 'em, Donnelly. What the hell happened here?"

I gave him a quick rundown on the matter, but since I didn't know anything, that only took a few minutes. Malloy took a look around but didn't come up with anything more than I had. The room was clean. No prints that didn't belong, no bloody footsteps, nothing.

There was one clue. An empty cash box lay on the floor with two rubber bands. It was unusual to see those any more. The war office had confiscated most of the rubber we could use and left us with staples and paper clips. The box was empty, of course. Whoever had killed Anderson looked to scram with the contents. With my investigation, I had to think that Anderson had stashed the diamond in the cash box and hidden it somewhere in the apartment. Maybe an accomplice had killed him and taken the ice for himself. There was no honor among thieves—and precious little in the police department.

The boys on the force had already written the robbery off as solved. Anderson had done it and been bumped off for the diamond. Sure, now they had a murder to solve, but I'd done what I'd been asked to do. I still didn't know how he pulled off the job. A conspirator would have made the heist that much easier. One could have kept Mrs. Van Hoskin occupied with wine and cheap flattery while the other made off with the jewels. The dame would have bought the line of someone like Anderson faster than a war bond.

So now all I had to do was figure out who his accomplice was.

Mrs. Van Hoskin had left me with two more names. The first was Agatha Day. She was something of a racing institution. No one seemed to remember who she was or how she'd made her entrance into racing society, but once in, she'd stayed with a vengeance.

Miss Day answered the door when I knocked. No servants here or fancy meetings for drinks. The old woman had to be eighty-five if she was a day, and she was still as sharp as a horseshoe tack. I only hoped that my remaining body parts would be in this good shape at her age.

She gave me a throaty laugh as I told her why I had come to see her. Not that she minded company. "I hate sitting around all the time these days, son. I seem to have outlived my contemporaries. The world is changing, and I wouldn't mind getting off."

I nodded and accepted her offer of tea. I would have preferred something stronger, but she didn't seem the type to offer liquor before teatime. And she didn't seem like the sort to steal diamonds, though she enjoyed the thought of being a suspect.

"I've seen a lot in my time. Men flying, two world wars. But I've never been accused of being a thief before. Are you going to give me the third degree or beat a confession out of me?"

I shook my head and tried to hide a smile. "No, ma'am. No such thing. I just need to ask you a few questions. Do you remember the necklace?"

"Sure, I do. Ethel Van Hoskin has more jewels than sense, for sure." A cough racked the old woman's body, but that didn't stop her from finishing the thought. "If you can believe it, she can't even buy a decent clasp for a million-dollar necklace." She tugged at the choker around her own neck. "I got this at Woolworth, and it's strong as a rope."

I looked at the necklace and had to agree that she was right. Nothing weak about that chain. I wondered why Mrs. Van Hoskin wouldn't have invested in a good clasp. Had someone played with the necklace before the party to create an opportunity to swipe the jewels? It seemed like a logical possibility. I wondered if Anderson had been invited to visit the Van Hoskins' estate before the party, giving him a chance to tamper with the necklace. But if that was the case, why not just take it then? Why go through the elaborate charade of stealing it at the party? I decided that the broken clasp had just been a fortunate break for the thief.

I told Miss Day about Anderson's murder, and she relished every detail.

"Well, I'll be. I've never been involved in a murder before. Is it like those little pocket books they have out?"

I shook my head. "The police seem to think that it was a falling out among the thieves. Though from what I've heard, it could have been a jealous boyfriend or husband."

"Ethel never was one for discretion. You only had to look at her jewels to know that she was all for show."

"So you think that Mr. Van Hoskin might have found out what was going on?" I started, but Miss Day pretended to look at the window and May's early sun. I didn't think that I'd learn much more from her, no matter what she knew, so I said my good-byes and went to my final interview.

The last person on my list was none other than Mr. Derby himself, Colonel Matt Winn. I had a hard time visualizing the guy behind all the recent improvements at the Derby as a jewel thief. But stranger things had happened.

Rumors were flying that 1944 might be the last year for the Derby if we didn't win the war. The shortages and the travel restrictions were catching up with America, and I'd heard grumbling that Roosevelt was going to ban horse racing if things didn't pick up soon. Losing the Kentucky Derby could be a powerful motive for needing ready cash. As it was, we were down to a "Streetcar Derby," since only people who were in the area could come to see it. That left sixty-odd thousand people who might want to help themselves to a few hundred thousand in hot jewels.

I'd seen the colonel a million times in the paper. Hell, who could go a May without seeing him all over? Still, I'd never met him. He was a tall, dapper man with white hair and a sophisticated air about him. I just couldn't see him sneaking down a hallway to heist a jewel. I'd seen too many criminals. I could usually tell just by looking at one of them.

The colonel was polite. Yes, he remembered the party. He'd seen the necklace, but he couldn't tell me much. Or so he said. I was beginning to doubt the word of everyone in town at this point. No one seemed to know a thing about the theft. I didn't even bother to ask about the murder.

* * *

That left me with a missing necklace, a dead man, and no answers. I tried to think like a killer, but that only brought back memories of the war. I'd ended up being the victim and not the killer. So that didn't buy me much insight.

I made a few phone calls to find out about the Van Hoskins' financial condition; the couple seemed sound as a rock. No reason for her not to buy a decent clasp for her necklace or pay a spud like me to find it.

I had started to see the light at the end of the race, when Mrs. Van Hoskin called. I agreed to visit her later and give her an update on the case, such as it was.

I drove up to the bluffs again. Some folks never got up there, but I'd visited twice in a week. I got to the estate and took the wide granite stairs two at a time. I wanted to get this interview over with and see if I could earn a fee. I didn't think I'd be making much from this case, even with the good intentions of my buddies on the force.

Mrs. Van Hoskin answered the door again. I was wondering if she was practicing for when there were servant rations or if she didn't want to be overheard. I entered behind her and followed her to the study. She'd lit a fire, and she collapsed on the floor in front of it without offering me a chair. I decided to stand.

"Have you found out anything?" Mrs. Van H wore what my ex-wife would have called a negligee. I just called it disgusting. Feathers covered the folds of flesh around her neck, but the dressing gown was pulled tightly around her ample décolletage, as she would have phrased it.

I nodded. "I have. Mark Anderson was murdered. The police contacted you?"

"Yes, that's awful. I don't know what to think. Was he killed for my diamond? I heard something about thieves falling out." Her eyes glittered as she spoke.

She seemed entranced by the danger that had come into her

life. I doubted that Mr. Van Hoskin provided her with much in the way of excitement. Most likely, he provided the dough and left her to her own amusements.

"He was killed for your diamond, Mrs. Van H, but not in the way that you mean."

Her face gave everything away before I said a word. She might have been a socialite, but she could never have played poker. "I don't know what you mean, I'm sure."

"Mark Anderson wanted something from you, but not the diamond. It would have been too hard to sell. He wanted cash, and you had a diamond." I looked around the room. She could have easily paid off a blackmailer, but I wondered how close Mr. Van H held the purse strings. Some dames never saw a penny of their husband's dough.

Her eyes widened and her mouth drooped at the corners. "I could never sell the Derby Diamond. It's been in my family for almost seventy years."

"I know. The diamond was never stolen. You just used that as an excuse to have me investigate Anderson. It gave a motive for his murder and a convenient scapegoat to look for—the missing accomplices. Who else besides you could have known the clasp would break and that you'd have to remove the necklace? The one time a year that you wore it in public. It was just a tad too convenient all along."

"I can assure you that no such thing happened." Her cheeks were still that rouged red, but the pallor of her skin had gone deathly pearl.

I started toward the door. "Well, even here, there are only so many places to hide a diamond necklace like that. The police shouldn't have too much problem finding it."

I left her sitting on the floor, crying, but I didn't feel too sorry for her. She'd have plenty of new clothes in prison.

The Kentucky Derby is more than a two-minute horse race during the first Saturday in May. It is the fulcrum of social affairs in the Kentucky-Southern Indiana region for many weeks preceding the race that the world watches. Preparation for "The Derby" blends all levels of society in one multifaceted goal.

Every local greenhouse forces tulips into bloom. Frenetic spring planting is done on public lands and in private gardens. Hundreds of galas, fetes, and parties—formal to very casual—are held in massive ballrooms, under huge tents, and in tiny family living rooms. Commercial and home kitchens have emitted the wonderful aromas of southern cooking for months. Derby products from T-shirts and incredible hats to Derby glasses and specially bottled Kentucky bourbon grace the aisles of every retail establishment within many miles.

Louisville's civic celebration spans the two- or three-week period before the race. The festivities begin with a seven-hour air show and the largest fireworks display in the United States, aptly called Thunder Over Louisville. The following days include a marathon, bed races, a balloon glow and race, a parade, a steamboat race on the Ohio River, and so much more.

A RUN FOR THE MOSES
by Tamera Huber

Tamera Huber is a screenwriter and published author. Her previous short story, "A Dish Served Cold," was published in Snitch. _She recently completed her first mystery novel,_ Void of Course. _In 2000, Tamera was awarded an Honorable Mention in the_ Writer's Digest _competition for the screenplay_ A Killing Moon. _She also pens feature articles for_ Louisville Magazine, Business First, _and_ Today's Woman Magazine.

"MOSES!" the old man said with the enthusiasm of a newly born-again soul.

Harrison Topper III looked at his grandfather-in-law and whispered, "Senile," to his wife, Sandra, as he fondled a six-inch-tall bobbling hula dancer.

She answered, "For years." Her face was permanently contorted into a frown. She stared in disgust at the plastic Hawaiian girl gyrating in front of her husband on the faux-marble dining table.

In her best attempt at sincerity, she said, "Tell us more, Papa," as if the thoroughly WASP family was from the old country.

Royden Pendrake studied the faces around the table. Their collective anticipatory stare begged for more information. Only Melissa seemed uninterested, playing with a three-inch rubber pig and a six-inch T. rex.

As a symbolic gesture of which she was well aware, Melissa occupied the chair farthest from Royden, her mother's father. The family patriarch was seated at the first of a pushed-together series of retro '50s tables. She hadn't wanted to come at all. Her fiancé, David, had persuaded her, as he often did, with arguments that would have made Clarence Darrow—and her grandfather— proud. Besides, even though she didn't know why, she wanted to make sure her grandfather was okay.

As the others clamored for the old man's attention like ants on stale bread, Melissa thought, *Let them suck up. I won't do it.*

Normally, Lynn's Paradise Café offered a fun, energy-filled atmosphere—and great food, in both quality and quantity. But the only food in the entire place, a succulent portion of beef ten-derloin, was in front of the host. No servers, no Lynn—just what remained of the Pendrake dynasty. No one really wanted to be at this family gathering.

He must have rented the place for the occasion, Melissa thought. A gargantuan feat for Derby Week, but the pretty blonde won-dered what was important enough to bring the family, who had barely spoken in years, together.

A sound from underneath the head table caught Melissa's attention. No one noticed when she bent down to investigate the noise. She viewed legs—table and otherwise—and a large, intricately woven basket with a hinged cover. The container's top bobbed up and down, reminding her of an old coffee percolator. She smiled and returned her attention to Lynn's table toys.

Contrary to the belief of some of his grandchildren, Royden's mind was anything but spent. Of the seven guests seated around the table, he respected only two—and one was his attorney and cousin once removed, M. Tyler Liggett, whom he didn't even like.

"You'll all be looking for Moses," Royden repeated. "It is an item that has been in the family for generations."

"I . . . but . . . what?" The comment/question originated from

Fred Pendrake. The diminutive 35-year-old still lived with his grandfather and presumed he always would.

"Yes, I know the trouble you have with the English language, my boy, but for pity's sake, don't attempt to speak it again in my presence."

"Shut up, Freddie," said an impeccably dressed man with unnatural blond hair and an insurable grin seated to Royden's right. John Wilson Pendrake was the oldest of the grandchildren and reeked of snake oil. "Let the man—I mean, Grandfather—speak."

Melissa drifted to a much different time. She was at Hampton Terrace again, the Pendrakes' rolling estate on the banks of the Ohio. She could see her grandmother in the distance, holding a palette and painting an Ohio Valley sunset. A cool breeze floated up from the water, kissing Melissa's cheek and blowing Grandma P's silver-kissed golden curls into her eyes. A much younger Grandpa Pendrake sat with 5-year-old Melissa on the porch swing overlooking the river.

She had learned to read by her grandfather's side on that weathered, wooden swing and wondered if it was still there. Sherlock Holmes was the detective du jour on that warm summer day. Melissa had loved the vacations that she spent with her grandparents, matching wits with Grandpa P and telling secrets to her grandmother. But she hadn't been back since her grandmother's funeral twenty years earlier.

A subterranean sound jolted Melissa's thoughts back to Lynn's. Royden pulled a sliver of his beef tenderloin and held it under the table before he continued. Melissa smiled, but the others were too busy thinking to notice.

"Derby Day. At the track," he said, as if everyone knew what he referred to. "You'll be looking for Moses. I'll be waiting in the family box. The first to bring the item to me wins." The nonchalant manner of his delivery masked the startling nature of the statement.

"Um. Wins what, exactly?" Harrison's salient interest was piqued nearly beyond his control.

"Ooh! Don't tell," said Freddie, clapping his hands together. "I love surprises."

"My millions," Royden continued. "My estate. Everything."

A rustling from beneath the table was the only sound in the restaurant.

"It's all or nothing, kids. My children are all gone." He shot a glance toward Melissa, who did not respond. "You're all that's left of the Pendrake line. I don't want to wait until I'm dead and have you fight over the things that Sarah and I loved. So . . . the one who finds my hidden treasure will get everything. The rest of you will receive one crisp, new dollar bill."

Royden fanned four Washingtons onto the tabletop for pure theatrical emphasis. Most of the participants shifted uneasily in Lynn's red vinyl chairs. Only Melissa smiled.

The old man signaled his attorney, and on cue, Liggett retrieved four documents from his imported leather attaché. "By the way, if anything happens to me before Derby Day, you are all disinherited. My current will leaves everything to the Kentucky Humane Society—everything except a dollar for each of you."

His revelation had the desired effect.

"Esquire here drew up the papers," he continued. "You will all sign, waiving your right to contest."

An objection rose in Sandra's face.

"Or you can leave now, a dollar richer."

Almost everyone looked to John for guidance. Other than Liggett and the patriarch, he was the oldest in the room—and the most resourceful. Although they would be locked in mortal combat for the old man's money soon enough, the others needed his skills.

"We all understand what you're doing," said John, the young Robert Redford look-alike.

"Do you?" Royden was amused.

"I think I speak for everyone when I say, Bravo!" John clapped his hands together for emphasis, which reminded Melissa of a seal juggling a rubber ball. "Well played," he added.

The old man's eyes narrowed.

"We know your fondness for games," John explained. "I respect that. But, really, having us traipse around a racetrack and its grounds on its busiest day. Couldn't we do something else? Draw straws? Duel?" He smirked.

Sandra and her husband let out a nervous laugh.

"John," Royden answered, "I can think of no better place for you than a horse stall."

The lips that held the million-dollar grin now quivered in anger.

"That's it." The old man rose from his chair with the help of a silver-headed cane. "Let the games begin."

No one moved.

"I said, you may go. Now!"

Liggett handed each departing grandchild a pen. Once each document was signed, the signatory was given a set of credentials that allowed access to all areas of the Downs on the first Saturday in May.

"But is it a statue?" Sandra asked. "A word? A photograph?" Her hands were shaking at the thought of all that money.

"Is it animal, vegetable, or mineral?" Freddie asked.

"Go! Now!" Royden ordered, and one by one they began to leave the restaurant. He noticed various degrees of bewilderment and determination on their faces as they filed out.

The fact that Melissa stayed surprised even her. Royden nodded for Liggett to leave.

"You didn't return my letters," said the old gentleman affectionately as he sat in the chair beside his granddaughter.

Cancer had slowly ravaged Melissa's mother the previous year.

The dying woman confessed that she had hidden letters that Grandpa P had sent to the young child. Melissa never knew what had happened between the father and daughter; she only knew, in the way that a child could, that her grandpa had forgotten her. Even though she now knew the truth, that old hurt lingered.

"I didn't—" Melissa began. "Mom thought I shouldn't see them. She never forgave you."

"You're wrong, Missy. During her last days, your mother and I spoke. What happened between us was unimportant. We forgave each other," he said. "Why can't you?"

Melissa sat motionless for some time.

"Why did you come?" he asked.

"Liggett sounded . . . it sounded urgent. I thought you might be—"

"Heavens, no. I'll be around for a long time yet."

"Oh," the woman said in a matter-of-fact manner, trying not to betray her genuine relief.

"Even if you don't want me in your life," he said, "my money would make things easier for you. You and that teacher, what's-his-name."

A bright red spread across her face. "David!"

"No disrespect meant." He laughed gently, reminding Melissa of earlier days. "Forgive me. My mind isn't as clear as it once was."

"How did you know about him?"

"*She* told me."

A quick change of subject was needed. Lacking another topic, Melissa said, "So, why a scavenger hunt?"

"You always liked to play games. Remember at Hampton Terrace? Word games, board games, puzzles. You loved anything that challenged your mind."

"And in between, we read Sherlock Holmes and Nancy Drew," she said.

Royden smiled and reached under the table. He lifted a brown-

and-black-spotted beagle pup from the basket by his feet. "His name is—"

"Bobby!" she shouted. Mr. Roberts, the beagle who'd had the run of her grandparents' grounds when Melissa was little, had the same markings. The 5-year-old girl had renamed the dog Bobby, after a popular teen idol.

The pooch jumped out of his master's hands and willingly into Melissa's arms. Royden was delighted and took the opportunity to move closer to his granddaughter.

"He comes from the same line. When I'm gone, he's yours, Missy. I know you'll take good care of him."

"Him . . . and a dollar," she mused.

"Solve the puzzle, my dear girl. I promise, you won't be sorry." He placed his hand on top of hers.

"I'm tired of playing," she said, returning the creature to his owner.

"I've been a stubborn man all my life. It's too late to make it up to your mother, but—"

Melissa shook her head.

"Just be there," he said. "Have faith in me."

Every part of her wanted to believe. "I'm glad you're okay." She stood and turned to leave, his words echoing behind her. *Faith? In him?*

She walked past the corncob art that decorated the southern side of Lynn's Paradise Café. Melissa loved the whimsy that the maize mural added to the building, even in its sad, vandalized state.

As she turned the key in the door of her 1990 Toyota, Melissa noticed a reflection of a man approaching her from behind. She swung around, adrenaline pumping.

"So. What were you and the old man discussing?" John asked.

"Old times," she replied.

He moved close enough to block the sunlight between them.

"Don't be coy. You were always his favorite. Did he give you inside information?" John asked.

"I was Grandmother's favorite, not his."

"Didn't like your mother much, did he? Well, Gram and Mom aren't here to protect you anymore. Are they?"

As John pressed closer to Melissa, she smelled the bourbon on his breath. When her cousin attained the desired effect, he laughed and backed away but only slightly. Melissa crossed her arms in front of her chest while she slid the car key between her fingers, ready to respond if he moved in again.

"Less competition would increase my chances considerably," John said. "Don't you think?"

As he drew near again, a squeal of tires startled the pair.

David emerged from the VW that he had parked an inch from John's kneecaps. He placed a hand tightly on the blond man's shoulder.

"Sir Galahad, I presume?" John laughed and slithered toward a waiting limousine.

"What are you doing here?" Melissa asked with both irritation and relief.

"You're welcome," the handsome, bookish man said. "I wanted to be here when you got out. What was that about?"

"John always liked drama," Melissa explained.

"So, what'd your gramps say?"

"Forget it. I don't want his money."

"I'm intrigued," said the dark-haired man.

"You're not going to believe this," she said.

The smell of mint leaves, tulips, and hay hung in the air surrounding the twin spires, as a yellow and orange sunrise peeked between the landmark towers. It was a chilly start, but the weatherman had predicted an 85-degree, cloudless day by the time the signature race ran. He also had a twenty on Gulliver's Quest, winner of the Florida Derby. Time would tell whether either prediction would be on the money.

Long before dawn broke, news crews were already in place. Reporters vied for backside interviews with the likes of Nick Zito, Bob Baffert, D. Wayne Lukas, and Pat Day.

Not wanting to lose a second of search time, Harrison, Sandra, and Freddie waited at Gate #17. It was only five-thirty in the morning, but a slightly inebriated infield crowd waited for the white iron gates to open at six o'clock. Harrison and Sandra had convinced Freddie to come with them. They assumed that if the slow-witted cousin was lucky enough to find the object, he could easily be duped. And if the Toppers found it first, the couple thought getting rid of Freddie would be even easier.

Sandra wore a wide-brimmed mauve hat with one large, blue ostrich feather leaning to the side. Her fuchsia dress suit clashed. Harrison sported a dapper white suit with a Panama hat.

Freddie had donned a professor-tweed jacket with blue jeans and a bewildered look. *Horses,* he thought. *I love horses.*

John Pendrake sat in a limo outside Gate #1. He refused to mingle with the throngs of people entering the track. He was above that. Besides, he was waiting. Melissa would be along soon.

The old man told her something, he reasoned. *I'll just follow my cousin's lead. Much more efficient that way.*

He had hired enough men to cover all the gates. They had photographs of Melissa and even David. The blond man patted the inside breast pocket of his jacket. He thought that the cold metal inside would ensure that he would end up with the money.

As the day moved along, the temperature warmed, pleasing not only the weather forecasters, but the crowd of racing patrons. Thousands of people poured through the freshly painted entrances.

Finally, John's patience was rewarded. After the second race, Melissa and David entered the gate where the limousine was parked.

"I'm going in just to tell him how ridiculous this is," Melissa said to her fiancé. "I won't go through hoops for that old man. He treated my mother like . . . lint. And now he's trying to make it up."

"Whoa! From what you told me, she gave as much as she got. And he did try to stay in touch. Right?"

"Maybe." Like her mother and grandfather, Melissa was stubborn.

"Cut him some slack, Mel. He's obviously trying to mend things."

"How? By having this stupid scavenger hunt? For Moses, of all things. One of my lunatic relatives will get millions. I just want. . . ."

David leaned in close to Melissa, gently touching her shoulders.

"I just want things the way they were," she said. "It was never about money before."

He held her and said, "Maybe he thinks that's the only way you'll come back."

"We could use the money," she said, "but I won't take it. Not like this."

"So? We'll be poor and happy," David said with a genuine smile. "There are worse things."

At a discrete distance, John surveyed his program—and the couple. *How touching.*

Sandra had trailed the same woman for nearly an hour. Harrison didn't understand why, and Freddie seemed oblivious, following her lead for lack of anything better to do. Along the way, they kept a lookout for any Moses-related paraphernalia.

Impeccably dressed, the woman they were shadowing wore a beige silk suit and a matching hat with a brown brim. When she settled into a seat in the Sky Terrace restaurant, Sandra signaled Harrison with a not-too-subtle head jerk.

"Say, Freddie," Harrison said, "why don't you check out the paddock? With all those horse owners and trainers, someone may have a portrait of Moses up in one of the stalls. Everyone can use a little divine help now and again."

"Great idea, Harry," Freddie answered.

Harrison cringed at the nickname that he had avoided all his life. After Freddie's departure, he asked his wife, "What if he finds something?"

"Wild-goose chase," she answered. "You remember when I said I was going to get a corn dog? I already looked."

"So, what's up?" her husband asked.

"I think I have it!"

"The woman in beige?"

"Yes."

"She's quite attractive, but I don't get it," Harrison said. "Why do you think—"

"Do you see what she's carrying?" asked Sandra.

"A day planner?"

"No, dear. It's a Bible. *The* Bible."

"And?" he asked.

"And the name Moses is in. . . ."

In unison, they said, "The Bible!" loud enough to interest passersby.

Shh! Sandra gestured.

"But isn't that a bit farfetched?" Harrison said a little quieter. "There could be any number of—"

"Don't you see? He'll have to give it to us even if it's not the exact thing he's looking for."

Harrison thought a while. "We'll need a plan," he finally said.

"I'm thinking."

"Me, too."

As the two thought and thought and thought, they continued to watch the unsuspecting missionary.

* * *

"You see him?" David asked Melissa.

"Since the gate," she answered. "Thinks he's slick."

"I have a plan," he said with a wink. He whispered into her ear, and the couple embraced.

For John's benefit, David pecked his fiancée on the cheek and said, "I'll see you at home, Mel."

Melissa filtered into the crowd and headed toward the cashier windows. David went in the opposite direction, turned beside the food concession, and rounded his way back to his original position. When John emerged from the back of a concrete pillar, David pulled him from behind by the collar of his Armani suit.

"May I help you?" David smiled.

John's maneuvering was skillful, but he failed at every attempt to negotiate his way around the determined human obstacle. "Think you're smart?" he asked.

"Only compared to you," David replied.

"How much do you pull a year as a teacher? I make 200K."

"But you're greedy. You want more, and you think Melissa can get it for you."

"She will. In one way or another," John said with a smirk. "Great body. I wouldn't mind—"

"Only through me." David stepped in *very* close to deliver the message.

Before John could pull out the silver object hiding in his breast pocket, a pair of Louisville's finest approached.

"Take it outside," said the larger officer.

John insisted, "I was just leaving."

David leaned contentedly against the pylon, as John exited.

The scents of horse manure, hay, sweat, and excitement filled the paddock area. Most spectators were interested only in the Derby horses. Not Freddie. He was on a mission.

The simple yet endearing man made his way to the individual stables' temporary quarters. He snuck or charmed his way into every tent. No Moses.

As he exited the last canvas tent, a kind voice asked, "May I help you?"

To Freddie's delight, he stood eye-to-eye with another man his size. "I really like horses. Um, have you seen a picture of Moses around here?" he inquired.

The jockey laughed. "No. Can't say that I have."

"So, what do you do?" The silk outfit, cap, and whip would have been the clue to others but was way over Freddie's head.

"I'm a jockey. About to run in the next race."

"How tall are you?" Freddie asked.

"Four-eleven."

"I'm an inch shorter! Do you think I could be a jockey?"

"Can't say, but there's no harm in trying. Come by the Meadow Farms tent after this race, and we'll talk."

I may not be smart enough to find Moses, Freddie thought, *but I think I've found my Promised Land.* "No more living at home," he said to the horse in the stall beside him. "No more handouts. I'm going to make it on my own."

Sandra peeked around a corner. The woman in beige had placed the Bible on the table in the Sky Terrace restaurant while she traveled through the buffet line.

"Here's our opportunity," Sandra said to her husband. "Before she gets back."

"Great. I'll cover you," he replied.

"Me? I was going to be the lookout for you."

"You look more innocent than I do," he insisted.

As the two continued to argue, the woman returned to the table.

"Okay," Sandra said. "You distract her, and I'll get the book."

"All right. I'll signal you. When I touch my finger to my nose, you grab it. Whatever you do, don't come until you see the signal." Harrison touched his nose for emphasis.

Sandra agreed.

The man in the Panama hat adopted his best upper-crust accent and soon joined the beige-clad woman at her table, pretending to be a long-lost acquaintance.

The two talked for what seemed to Sandra to be an inordinately long time. But she stuck to the plan and waited for the signal. And waited. And waited.

Melissa negotiated millionaires of every shape and size, businessmen and women in suits, celebrities, and celebrity-hunting local reporters and fans.

Finally, she reached Royden's box. The silver-headed cane that her grandfather normally carried lay askew on one of the chairs, but its owner was gone. As she approached, Melissa noticed the old man's beagle peering from a basket hidden underneath one of the chairs. The pup jumped out and ran into her arms.

A twangy voice came from the box above. "If you're looking for the old gent," said the man in the lime green leisure suit with the $5,000 watch, "he's gone. With a young guy, about your age. Reminded me of some pretty-boy actor—or con man. Didn't seem like the older feller wanted to go. They were acting a might strange."

He pointed to the beagle in Melissa's arms. "And that there pooch you're holding made quite a fuss. Bit the younger guy's hand. I was always partial to dogs myself. I put him back in his basket so no one would throw him out. Kept an eye on him for the old man."

"Did you see where they went?" Melissa asked.

"No, but the younger one said something about getting Moses—maybe hoses—from him. What on earth?"

The puppy looked up and whimpered to Melissa.

"Thanks for taking care of him," she said.

"He looks like a George to me."

Melissa grabbed the cane and basket and ran toward the nearest exit into the breezeway while she held the pup underneath her blouse. She found David waiting at their predetermined spot next to a cashier's window.

"I just saw your grandfather with that creep cousin of yours," he said.

"Why didn't you stop them?"

"Um, well. . . ."

"Never mind. We have to hurry!"

"What is it?"

"We've got to get ahead of them," she said, breathing hard. "I'll explain on the way."

Sandra's patience was exhausted. Harrison and the woman in the beige outfit had been chatting and laughing for two hours. Strains of "My Old Kentucky Home" could be heard from the infield. *Maybe he forgot the signal,* Sandra reasoned. *That must be it.*

She slid over to the table where her husband and the Bible-toter were comfortably seated, then nonchalantly dropped to the floor. Crawling on her hands and knees through bits of fallen lettuce and mint leaves, she made her way under the table's skirt as her blue feather peeked out from under the white linen.

She felt around with her fingers. A fork. *No, that's not it.* A napkin. Finally she felt the leather of the Good Book under her probing fingertips. But she couldn't budge it. A heavy weight prevented her from moving the object.

As Sandra raised her head from underneath the table to evaluate the obstacle, she noticed that the warm May sun was blocked and a silhouetted policeman hovered over her.

"That's her, Officer!" the Bible owner said with a thick European accent. "She's been following me around all day." The woman waved Harrison closer. Clinging to his arm, she added, "This kind gentleman was good enough to warn me about her."

"Poor creature," Harrison said. "Escaped from a mental ward, I expect."

"Harrison!" screamed Sandra.

"Who?"

"I'm your wife! Sandra!"

"Obviously delusional." He shook his head in sympathy for the lost soul.

"You said you'd never leave me."

Harrison leaned close to her and whispered, "And you said you'd be rich someday."

Sandra began to shout at him, but the policeman came between the couple.

"What the. . . ." The officer pointed to the track and said, "If that don't beat all!"

Trailing the Derby horses that had just crossed the finish line was Freddie, dressed in silks and mounted on a Thoroughbred. His grin was wider than the gap between himself and the bona fide jockeys. Brown-shirted sheriff's deputies who had obviously trained for just such an occurrence used their equestrian skills to overtake the late Derby entry.

Sandra smiled, momentarily forgetting her husband and the Bible lady.

"Are you going to come quietly now?" the officer asked.

She kept her smile and held her head in the highest Southern belle tradition. "Of course." She glared a last dagger at Harrison and his new acquisition.

After the officer led Sandra away, Harrison embraced Lady Carlisle's delicate hand. "I'm so glad you're all right," he said. "I never would have forgiven myself if anything had happened to such a beautiful"—he kissed her hand and continued—"and intelligent woman."

She blushed and said, "Pardon me, Mr. Jenkins, but perhaps we could have dinner? I'm staying at the Brown. Room 301. Tonight? Nine?"

"I'll be there, Lady Carlisle."

She smiled. "Call me Andrea. Titles don't mean much here in America."

"And, uh, don't forget this," Harrison said as he picked up the Bible.

She opened it. Instead of text from the prophets, the book was hollowed out and contained an outrageously gaudy diamond necklace.

He almost hyperventilated at the sight. "Exquisite."

"Yes. You are," she replied.

Melissa and David ran at a dead heat and managed to out-flank John and Royden. The couple turned to face the two men.

"Don't get in my way, coz," John said as he jabbed a cylindrical metal object into his grandfather's ribs.

"Don't hurt him!" Melissa screamed.

The beagle pup jumped out of her arms and barked fiercely, distracting John. David wrestled with the wayward cousin as the dog nipped at John's ankles. A silver object fell from John's hand and clanked on the floor. Instead of a gun, a long, metal cigar case bounced on the concrete.

"Why, you. . . . Holding me up with a cigar case?" said Royden. The old man took a swing at John, but his balance was minimal without the cane, and he fell.

One of the four police officers alerted by the scuffle helped him off the floor. Once Melissa, David, and Royden explained the situation, the officers agreed to place no charges against them if they would leave—immediately.

As the men in blue escorted John to a police cruiser, he struggled and shouted. "What was it?" he screamed. "I have to know. Where was it? I *must* know!"

Royden just smiled and looked at Melissa and his faithful companion. "Look at the dog tag, Missy," he said in an extremely kind tone.

She picked up the beagle and read aloud, "If found, return Moses to Royden Pendrake." She looked at the old man. "I have a confession to make, Grandpa P," Melissa said. "I saw his tag that night at Lynn's. I knew he was the treasure you wanted us to find."

David stared at her. "You what?"

"Thanks, Missy," said Royden. "You saved me." He held out his arms, and his granddaughter filled them.

Moses squealed, crushed by the embrace.

"Sorry, little guy," Melissa said. "I think I'll call him Moze. Much more hip."

"I'll have Liggett do the paperwork for the estate. You're rich, my dear."

Melissa looked at David. He nodded.

"No hurry, Grandpa P. Why don't you come home with us for dinner? It's just David and me, nothing fancy."

"I'd like that," Royden said.

As they passed the tulip-filled center court, the trio spotted Sandra. She had eluded her captors and was chasing Harrison and Lady Carlisle with a shrimp fork she had grabbed from the restaurant.

Secretariat, perhaps the greatest racehorse of the 20th century, was foaled in Virginia at Meadow Farms Stable on March 30, 1970. The sire was Bold Ruler and the dam was Somethingroyal. The beautiful red chestnut colt was almost perfect—a sturdy barrel chest, perfect legs with three white socks, and a star on his forehead.

Dubbed "Big Red" by the media, Secretariat was one of eleven Thoroughbreds to win the Triple Crown. He was voted Horse of the Year as a 2-year-old and again as a 3-year-old. Starting twenty-one races, he won sixteen, and his exhibitions of speed and stamina thrilled millions and gave a huge boost to horse racing in the 1970s. During the first part of his 3-year-old season, Claiborne Farm syndicated the colt for a then-record $6.08 million.

The 19-year-old stallion was euthanized October 4, 1989, to end his painful suffering from laminitis. A necropsy was performed after his death, and Secretariat's heart, while normal pathologically, was almost twice the size of a normal equine heart.

WALKING AROUND MONEY
by Beverle Graves Myers

＊

Beverle Graves Myers is currently working on a series of historical mysteries set in the decadent world of 18th-century Venice. Her novel Interrupted Aria *was released in April 2004 by Poisoned Pen Press, and a short story in the same series will appear in an upcoming issue of* Alfred Hitchcock's Mystery Magazine.

CALL IT SEMI-RETIREMENT. Or keeping my hand in. Retirement just has too final a ring about it. Dull, lonely. Like the thud the lid of Ruby's casket made when the preacher closed her up for the ride to the cemetery.

That's mainly why I kept working. The house just seemed so empty. You're married to someone for thirty-five years and suddenly she's gone, all on account of a pea-sized tumor so deep in her head that no scalpel could reach it. That's what her doctor'd told me. Nice young fella.

When Ruby closed her eyes for good, he'd put his hand on my shoulder and said, "Don't shut yourself up in grief, Pete. You need to be around people. Work if you're able, or take up a hobby."

Well, I was never much for hobbies. My work had been my hobby for more years than I wanted to count. Sure, I'd had to slow down. Make adjustments. There'd been a lot of days when my arthritis laid me so low that I couldn't even button my shirt or knot my tie. But I wasn't exactly ready for the glue factory.

Besides, I had to work. My job wasn't too sweet where retirement benefits were concerned. Don't get me wrong; I had enough set aside for the basics. But a fella needs some walking around money.

So there I was on the first Saturday in May—Derby Day to the good folks in Louisville, Kentucky—scanning the crowds that had gathered for the horse race that some joker had dubbed "the greatest two minutes in sports." That always gave me a pain. Where's the sport in a bunch of horses running around a track with five-foot midgets holding on for dear life? Give me the Super Bowl, any day. Football—now there's a game.

Anyhoo, to me, the Derby's always seemed like a good excuse to celebrate the return of leafy trees and sunny days. A giant springtime frolic to make everyone forget the gray Kentucky winter.

And I do mean everyone.

College kids didn't mind waiting in line all night to lug coolers and blankets into the infield to drink and party. High above, next to the famous twin spires spearing the cloudless blue sky, businessmen entertained clients in the spiffy confines of Millionaires Row. In between, it was packed boxes and a slew of people cramming as close to the rails as they could get.

I chuckled as guys who only came to the track once a year tried to argue odds like they were veteran handicappers. The women were good for a few laughs, too—showing off new outfits and hats piled with everything from flowers to blinking lights. One doll even had her head rigged out like a miniature Churchill Downs, with plastic spires poking up from the crown of her straw hat and toy horses circling the wide brim. She kept pestering the roving TV reporter to put her on camera, but the girl with the mike was too busy chasing celebrities.

And then, the grifters and dippers came to the track to prey on the lot of 'em.

That's where I came in. It was my job to keep an eye out for wallets and purses that strayed into the wrong hands.

It was only the second race of the day, a few hours before the strains of "My Old Kentucky Home" would kick off the Derby horses' parade to the starting gate, but people had been pouring into the track since early morning. My post near the stairs in the third-floor grandstands gave me a good view. Not of the horses, but of the strutting, stumbling, shoving crowd that constantly milled from seats to betting windows.

If anybody would take time to give me the once-over, they'd see a skinny, balding man who'd let his gut "dunlop," dressed in a white, open-collar shirt, baggy gray slacks, and a cheap sports coat. The kind of guy who asked for a comb-over at the barbershop even though his nine or ten gray hairs didn't come close to covering his shiny scalp. But no one paid me any attention. I looked like hundreds of other losers who haunted the track, hoping to win the big one whether it was Derby Day or not.

I slouched against the wall—pain not too bad thanks to the warm day and the pills that young doc had given me—and pretended to study the *Daily Racing Form*. That's when I spotted her.

Attractive broad, but in an understated kind of way. Her cream-colored pantsuit was quality but not eye-catching, and her hair straddled the line between blonde and light brown. It was swept up under a close fitting cap. Beret? Tam? Whatever they call those things, it matched her jacket and pants. She looked like a tall, thin vanilla soda edging through a throng of strawberry sundaes and banana splits loaded with cherries and whipped cream.

I wasn't sure at first. She didn't exactly fit the profile. Maybe she wasn't cruising the crowd for easy marks; maybe she was just looking for somebody. Then she cozied up behind a red-faced guy in khakis, golf shirt, and navy blazer—a fraternity boy gone to seed, working on his fourth or fifth mint julep. On the alert now, I slipped the racing form in my pocket. Still, I hesitated.

Know what gave me the final tip-off? No jewelry. Oh, she had some little gold balls in her ears, but no rings, no watch, no bracelets. Nothing that could snag when she snaked that slim wrist into a bag or under a jacket.

Down on the dirt, the second race was coming to a fighting finish. A horse stumbled, and the caller's monotone voice shot up an octave. All eyes turned to the track.

I was already moving when my vanilla lady slipped two fingers under frat boy's blazer and lifted the wallet from his back pocket. In one graceful motion, she folded the wallet into her program and made a half-circle turn to head for the stairs.

I was right behind her, but the crowd was tight. Someone shoved me into that pesty woman with the giant racetrack hat, who promptly squealed and ground a stiletto heel right into my big toe. I let a few choice words fly and hobbled after my dipper on a throbbing foot.

The lady with the hijacked wallet was really moving, weaving in and out of the throng like an All-American halfback, but I knew the Downs better than she did. While she was stymied by a crowd at the bottom of the stairs, I cut through a corner refreshment stand and caught up with her on the pavement by the paddock.

"Excuse me, ma'am." I latched a firm hand under her elbow. "But I'll have to ask you to come with me."

She jerked her arm, eyes blazing. "Get your hand off me."

I kept that hand where it was and used my other to open my jacket and flash an ID with a gold badge pinned to it. "Track security, ma'am. Let's not make this any harder than it has to be."

Her nostrils flared, but she smoothed her pink lips into a pleasant smile. "There must be some mistake, Officer." She gave that last word a flirtatious lilt.

She was going to try a bluff; somehow I wasn't surprised. I just hoped she hadn't passed the wallet to a partner. I made her for a solo act, but you can never be sure.

"No mistake," I said. "I was right behind you when you lifted that guy's wallet on the third tier."

She made something between a snort and a giggle and used the tip of her folded program to wipe a stray wisp of hair off her forehead. "I'm sure I don't know what you're talking about."

She gazed at me with smoke gray eyes, a bit crinkled around the edges. She wasn't as young as I'd first thought. The way she smiled and cocked her head kind of reminded me of my Ruby. I'd met her at the track, too, about a hundred years ago.

I cleared my throat. "The wallet's right there, ma'am. In your program."

"What if you're right?" She lowered her voice to a throaty whisper, not that the crowd streaming around us was paying any attention. "What do you intend to do about it?"

"I'm going to walk you down to the police post at the front gate. If you won't come willingly, I'll have to call someone to convince you." Tightening my grip on her elbow, I used my free hand to press a switch on the walkie-talkie attached to my belt. It crackled ominously.

She looked away, then back into my eyes. She clutched the program to her chest and let her shoulders slump. "Could you . . . give me a minute? Just let me explain?"

I hesitated a breath, then steered her over to a relatively quiet spot under a columned arcade wedged between the building and the grandstand garden. The midday sun beat down on the tiny patch of grass while red and yellow tulips in curving beds waved their heads in the gusty breeze.

"Okay," I said, not letting go of her elbow. "You've got my attention, but this had better be good. Believe me, I've heard 'em all."

The corners of her mouth drooped and the crinkles around her eyes seemed to deepen. "Then I'm sure you've heard this one. It's an old story—a sick relative."

I rolled my eyes. "Poor old granny needs an operation?"

"No, poor young brother has AIDS. His lungs are shot and he's puking up blood." She jerked her arm from my hand. Red sprang to her pale cheekbones.

"That's rough." I stretched my arm to the column to my right and shuffled my feet a few inches to the left so she couldn't duck out from under me. "Don't they have medicine for that now?"

"There's medicine—if you've got the money. Bobby needs over a dozen different drugs; his insurance pays for six. We're fighting them, but while they come up with more forms for him to file, the money's got to come from somewhere."

"Ever try working? A regular paycheck does wonders for your bank account."

Her smoky eyes hardened to flint. "I work every day. Teaching second grade, as a matter of fact. And if you think a teacher's salary can keep up with the latest brand-name drugs, then you've never had someone you love at the mercy of the doctors and the insurance companies."

I wanted to tell her I knew all about it, that the cancer drugs that Ruby'd had to take by the handful were no cheaper than drugs for AIDS. But I didn't. I just stared at her, thinking, working my jaw back and forth.

She mistook my silence for sympathy and raised a bit of a smile. "Can't we work this out? If I get arrested, I'll lose my job and won't be able to help Bobby."

She brushed a few honey-colored strands off her forehead, slipped the wallet out of the program, and held it out to me. "Couldn't you just return this? Tell the man up in the grandstand that he dropped it and you picked it up?"

I didn't answer.

"I promise you'll never see me here at the track again. Never." Then she widened those gray eyes and cocked her head in that way she had that reminded me of Ruby. Brother or no brother, this was one classy lady. I found myself accepting the wallet and placing it firmly in my jacket pocket.

She looked like she didn't quite believe I'd fallen for it, but she whispered her thanks and made a tentative gesture toward my arm that was still blocking her in. Before I could move, squeals of excitement rang out and the crowd shifted toward the clubhouse entrance.

A hefty teenager in pink overalls vaulted over the tulips, screaming, "Oh my gosh, it's Kid Rock."

Several dozen of her friends followed. I bobbed to my tiptoes. All I saw was a dirty, mop-headed character that could've been a skid row bum surrounded by big guys in black leather jackets.

I turned back to my now-smiling dipper. "Kid Who?" I asked.

"Kid Rock. He's a pop singer. All the rage."

We both shook our heads, equally bewildered by the whims of the younger generation. Then she was weaving gracefully through the crowd, her back straight and head high, hurrying toward the nearest exit.

I blew a sigh through rubbery lips. Second-grade teacher—what a crock!

She was a pretty fair dipper, though. Course, she didn't have a patch on me when I was in my prime. Like back in 1969, the year Majestic Prince battled Arts and Letters neck and neck down the front furlong. Back then, my fingers had been as quick and nimble as a spider spinning a web. I'd cleared over $3,000 while the punters were pounding the rails and screaming at the horses. Now my arthritic hands couldn't lift a baby bottle off a sleeping infant without getting busted.

It was quite a comedown—bleeding the dippers instead of making the dip myself—but a man's gotta do what a man's gotta do. The light bill needs to be paid, stiff fingers or not. At least I was still working.

Keeping a sharp eye out for the real track security, I headed for the nearest men's room to retrieve my loot. I didn't mess with credit cards, and it'd be stupid to keep the guy's wallet with all his ID. The folding money, that's what I was after.

The place was packed, guys standing ten deep to use the urinals. No problem for me. The more people around, the fewer individuals get noticed. The smell was a lot to put up with, though. One guy had puked up a toiletful that would have gagged a maggot. Trying not to breathe, I waited till a stall opened up, then closed myself inside to transfer the bills into the money belt I kept strapped around my waist. When I came out, I'd wash my hands, slip the wallet in a wad of damp paper towels, and dump it in the trash. Then on to the next dipper who thought he'd ride the Kentucky Derby gravy train.

Ha! Old Pete was ready and on his mark to hijack that train.

That's when it hit me. Surrounded by the slick, metal walls of that restroom stall, I felt like I could've been shut up in the casket with Ruby. My lungs were sucking away at the foul air, and my heart was hammering at my chest. Suddenly, I knew I was looking at endless days filled with bad coffee, too many cigarettes, and too much Oprah on TV. It was time to retire, like it or not.

You see, that lady was good, after all. Real smooth. When I reached in my inside pocket, the wallet wasn't there. She'd double-dipped me. Grabbed that fat wallet when I'd turned to look at Kid What's-his-name. And I hadn't had a freaking clue.

Princess Margaret and her husband, Lord Snowden, were official guests for the 100th Derby on May 4, 1974. They arrived in Lexington, Kentucky, on Friday, May 3 (Derby Eve), and were the guests of C. V. and Mary Lou Whitney. Since this was an official State visit, the British government paid the costs of the trip. The Royal couple arrived with thirty-eight pieces of luggage. They spent the rest of the day touring horse farms and attending a private Derby Eve dinner party hosted by the Whitneys.

The same day, the U.S. Post Office announced that it would issue a ten-cent commemorative stamp showing ten colts rounding the bend at Churchill Downs.

On Derby Day, Princess Margaret and Lord Snowden entered the track at Churchill Downs in a motorcade coming from the stable area, crossing the backstretch and circling the track. They viewed the Derby from the Winner's Circle pagoda across from the grandstand. The Derby was run to a cheering crowd of 163,628 fans. Cannonade, who had won the Opening Day Stepping Stones race, won the Derby by two lengths over Hudson County.

Murder Under the Stars
by Elaine Munsch

————✦————

Elaine Munsch is a native of Cleveland, Ohio, but has ties to the bluegrass on her maternal grandfather's side dating back to the American Revolution. She began her lifelong career as a bookseller at the aptly named Readmore Books in Louisville and has been a Barnes & Noble manager for over a decade. She has taught classes on the mystery genre and currently is president of the Ohio River Valley Chapter of Sisters in Crime. Elaine and her husband, Charles, live with their cat, Murphy, in Louisville. Their daughter, Kristin, lives in Chicago with her guinea pigs, Sam and Cokie.

IT WAS A GRAND NIGHT FOR MURDER. As Silky Sullivan sang, she glanced out over the audience of selected guests of Paige Browning. They were enjoying the soft sounds of "Silky Sullivan and the Schumacher Five," one of two bands providing the evening's entertainment. Silky knew she had the audience in her hand; they dreamily gazed at her. Mrs. Browning was sure to be pleased with the way the evening was going. The breeze was gentle, the music soft, the food and drink flowing, and the guests purring.

At "Murder Under the Stars," as Mrs. Browning had entitled her charity gala, not only would the guests eat and dance, they would also be participating in a murder mystery, carefully tailored to fit the '40s theme the hostess preferred. Although this was not the largest of the pre-Derby parties, those who attended were the crème de la crème. Or at least that was what Silky assumed, since a table for eight cost $10,000, with only six guests at each table. The two remaining seats were filled with actors from the "Murder on Call" troop.

Everyone attending had been asked if they wanted to participate in the setup or in the solving of the crime. The guests who were joining the cast for the evening received a red Derby rose boutonniere so everyone would know that their actions were probably part of the play and most likely not intended to cause offense.

In their spacious backyard, the Brownings had set up a small stage and dance floor, with the feel of a nightclub, where the performers and guests could mingle, dance, and, of course, "die."

Silky turned slightly as she sang "Stairway to the Stars," checking with Bill—her pianist, arranger, and conductor—so she would know if he thought they should end with the next song or continue. Silky relied upon him to either cut or extend the set depending on how the audience reacted. Bill raised three fingers from the keyboard and nodded to her. She smiled back. She was feeling as mellow as the songs she sang.

When their set was over, the Schumacher Five yielded the stage to the other band. Refreshments awaited in a small parlor set aside for the bands.

As Silky stepped down onto the dance floor, Mrs. Browning signaled to her. The hostess took her hand, thanking her for such a wonderful beginning to the evening. The handsome gentleman to the right of Mrs. Browning added his praise by asking Silky to dance with him.

Mrs. Browning smiled a matchmaker's smile and said, "Silky, please oblige this rascal nephew of mine so he will stop pestering me for an introduction. Silky, this is Artie Goodman from Benchmark, Kentucky. Artie, this is Silky Sullivan. Now shoo."

Artie had the grace to blush as his aunt pushed them onto the dance floor. Since he was wearing a red rose, Silky put on her best imitation of a shy Rosemary Clooney.

"So, Mr. Goodman, what brings you from the little town of Benchmark to the bright lights of Louisville?"

"Aw, Miss Sullivan," he drawled. "Please call me Artie. And it was the opportunity to meet you that dragged my weary bones all the way up here. I will say that it was worth every bump in the road so I could finally gaze into those baby-blue eyes of yours." He cocked his head, giving her a sly grin.

"If your footwork is as smooth as your tongue," she said, "we'll have a great dance. Are you related to the great Benny Goodman, by any chance?"

"Only if you mean my brother, and he doesn't have a musical gene in him, unlike myself, who, as you can tell by my dancing, possesses more than a modicum of talent." With that he swung her around with a step or two worthy of Fred Astaire.

Silky responded with a Ginger-like tap step. "Please tell me that there aren't more at home like you."

"As a matter of fact, there are four of us—Artie, Benny, Charlie, and Danny. Father thought it would be fun to alphabetize his children; he was the town's librarian, and everything had to be organized. Mother had the good sense to stop him at four children rather than trying for the full alphabet."

"Well, look at the bright side. At least he didn't give you call letters." Silky laughed and then pulled back from his arms. "Or did he?"

"No, thank goodness. Though that might have been fun; I wonder how he would have classified us." He drew her back to him. "And, now, tell me, Miss Sullivan, were your parents horse crazy or just crazy to name you after a Derby horse, and a loser, no less."

"I'll have you know that I was baptized Sylvia Ann Mary

Margaret, so as not to miss any female relative with a bit of money to be left to her niece. My granddad, who definitely would have been classified under 'railbird,' stuck me with my nickname. He thought I was so precious that I should be wearing silk diapers, not cotton. And alas, Silky it was to be."

The dance ended and Artie bowed and winked.

Silky curtsied gracefully, spreading her chiffon skirt with a flourish. "I'd better scoot. Thank you for the dance." She tapped the red rose. "I hope you enjoy the play."

As she was about to turn and leave, a loud argument broke out on the other side of the dance floor. An older woman, dressed to the nines in white and dark blue spangles, was pushing and shouting at a younger woman. All Silky could make out was something about "if you think you are going to steal him, you are wrong, wrong, wrong." To accentuate each *wrong*, she gave an emphatic push that gained in strength each time, almost knocking the younger woman into the table next to the floor.

Artie said to Silky, "Excuse me, I'm on now. Artie to the rescue." And he hurried to the women, separating them.

Silky thought about staying to watch the drama unfold, but her stomach rumbled. She remembered all those finger sandwiches, snacks, and libations that Mrs. Browning had so graciously provided in the parlor. Joining her band, she snagged a sandwich and a bottle of water, looking mournfully at the dessert tray. If she wanted to wear this dress more than once, she needed to watch her figure.

Bill, who watched her figure for her and didn't need to watch his, sat next to the sweets table, obviously having had his way with it. Fred and Sam, drum and bass players respectively, played cards, their dirty dishes on the table next to them. Jim, the saxophonist, and Jeremy, the trumpet player, were outside smoking.

"It's going really well, isn't it guys?" she asked. "We'll get a few more gigs from this."

Bill nodded. "We may not get paid a lot tonight, but I've had two inquiries already about parties. Cracking the Derby party scene can only mean good things."

He knew Silky didn't care about the "big break"; she just liked to sing and dress up like they did in all those '40s comedies and musicals. A little song, a little dance, and snappy repartee. Silky belonged to another era.

The object of his thoughts was doing the few stretches allowed by the blue number she was wearing. When she turned to him, Bill said, "Let's take a turn around the house. I don't want to go outside while the play is going on."

The pair left the parlor and walked upstairs to the second floor. The house, a standard rectangle, was mansion-size more than bungalow-size. They strolled along, admiring the artwork on the walls and the floral arrangements thoughtfully placed on the tables, then descended the staircase at the far end of the main hallway.

From the parlor, Jeremy stuck his head out of the door. "Hey, guys, Mrs. B. was just here. She says we have about twenty minutes until the murder. We're going out to watch. Want to join us?"

"Go ahead," Bill said. "We'll be along in a minute."

Silky peeked into the rooms where the doors had been left ajar. When she spotted the drawing room door open, she pulled Bill inside. There were fireplaces at either end, each with a dark wooden mantel. The room, dimly lit with crystal oil lamps on the mantels, was decorated as Silky imagined an English drawing room would be. Soft, green-striped wallpaper with shades of cream; pale gold swags over the windows. The furniture was probably mahogany, very formal and uncomfortable looking, with the cloth reflecting the shades of green, cream, and gold. Elegant oriental rugs with the carefully placed furniture broke the room into several small groupings, making for cozy conversation. A baby grand piano complemented the furnishings.

"What a beautiful room," Silky said as she twirled around, breaking into "I Could Have Danced All Night."

Bill slid onto the piano bench and tickled the ivories lightly. Silky stepped closer to one of the fireplaces to inspect the large painting of a young Paige Browning that hung over the mantel. Leaning forward, she spotted a small evening bag, white silk with midnight-blue beading done in intricate swirls, tucked behind one of the oil lamps. Nobly thinking of returning it to its rightful owner, she opened it and found what she would later describe as a "darling little gun, surely just a cigarette lighter."

"Hey, Bill, look at this. Remember the lighter my granddad had?"

Bill had barely time to look up when Silky flicked the hammer, expecting a lighted wick to appear. Instead, a bullet roared past him, exploding a vase containing the requisite red Derby roses.

"Oh, Bill! Are you all right?"

"What the devil are you doing, Silky? Don't you know anything about guns?"

"What gun? I thought this was a lighter." She placed the offending weapon on the mantel as she headed toward the mess of roses and water on the rug. "What am I going to tell Mrs. Browning? It's going to take me years to pay for the vase, let alone rebuild all the goodwill I just destroyed." She bent over to pick up the roses and the pieces of the vase. "Bill, find a towel or something so I can mop up this water. Pleeease."

He sighed and headed for the door, only to be stopped by a shriek from Silky.

"I can't believe it, Bill! I've killed someone."

"Silky, what the hell are you talking about. You can't kill anyone with a derringer unless you stick it in their ear. And *my* ear is the only thing that bullet came close to clipping. It's probably just a prop for the murder mystery."

He had reached her side, and they both stood over the body. It was the older woman Silky had seen on the dance floor. Bill grimaced but bent down to take a better look, hoping he was right. Much to his chagrin, when he touched the body, he could tell this was not a prop. When he tried to find a pulse, he knew the woman was dead.

"I think we can rule out being asked to play for any of Letitia Wentworth's parties," he said. "Unless I'm wrong, that is who this is. But not by your hand, unless she died of a heart attack when she heard the shot. You'd better get Mrs. Browning, or the police, and call for an ambulance—not necessarily in that order."

Silky's shoulders slumped and she tossed the roses aside. What a rotten night this was turning out to be. *Mrs. Browning should be fetched first,* she thought. *It's her house, after all.*

She found Mrs. Browning at her table with her husband, Richard, and the nephew, Artie.

"Mrs. Browning, there's a problem in the drawing room," she said in a serious but not alarming tone. "I think you and your husband should come with me."

The three stood up; Artie obviously included himself in the solution to this problem.

As she led the trio back to the drawing room, Silky tried to stammer out exactly what she and Bill were doing in the room . . . and how she opened the purse . . . and fired a shot from a gun . . . and least of all, at this point, shattering what was probably a Waterford vase . . . but, in hopes of putting a positive spin on the events, finding the dead body. A good hostess would not want a body just lying around undiscovered, would she?

An answer to that came in the form of a withering scowl from Mrs. Browning just as they joined Bill in the drawing room. Artie took Silky's hand and advised her to be quiet before she was sent out of the room for misbehaving. She sat on the piano bench, close enough to hear but out of striking distance. What Silky heard made her glad she had withdrawn.

"That stupid bitch of a sister! She said she'd ruin my party. And now she has."

Letitia Wentworth was Paige Browning's sister? thought Silky. *And not a close one.*

Richard Browning pulled his wife away, tut-tutting and mumbling about how distraught she was.

Artie bent close to examine the late Letitia. He suddenly pulled back and said, "Cyanide."

"What are you talking about?" asked Bill.

"Smell the bitter almonds?" Artie asked.

Bill bent down, sniffed, and nodded.

I used to love almonds, thought Silky as she remembered her favorite cake, *though this might throw me off desserts for a while. Should I ever work again, at least I'll be able to wear this dress.*

Richard approached Bill and Artie and said, "She was poisoned? How?" His wife and Silky joined them.

"My guess would be in her last drink," Artie said, peering under furniture for the offending beverage.

They all looked around, Silky reaching for the julep glass under a nearby chair, when, for the second time that evening, Artie grabbed her hand. "Fingerprints, Miss Sullivan."

"Right," she peeped, retreating to the piano bench.

The others huddled, whispering.

From her perch, Silky glanced at the purse on the mantel then the dress worn by Letitia. She walked to the purse and carried it to the huddle. "Mrs. Browning, is this your sister's purse? It would seem to match her dress."

"Probably." And she turned back to the huddle.

"Why did she have a loaded gun?" asked Silky.

With that question, all eyes turned to Silky.

"I mean, did she usually carry a gun? And why bring it to a party? What part in the murder play did she have? Did it call for a gun? Which still begs the question of why it was loaded."

Mrs. Browning scowled again at Silky. "She probably brought it to ruin my party by killing that trollop that her husband, Robert, was parading around all night. Unless she intended to kill her husband. Maybe she was going to kill both of them. Maybe she—"

Richard moved her away, hushing her.

Bill broke the silence. "Shouldn't we be calling the police?"

"NO!" shouted Mrs. Browning. "I'll not have them ruining my party. Letty is dead and she'll stay that way. We'll wait until the party is over. Artie, aren't you some sort of policeman in Benchmark? Can't you be in charge until the guests leave?"

"Aunt, I think Bill is right. I'm a full-time librarian and only a part-time deputy at the sheriff's office. Hardly qualifications for stalling a real police investigation."

"A librarian, a policeman, *and* a dancer." Silky smiled. "A regular renaissance man, Artie. When our dance finished and you left, saying you were 'on' now. Was that part of the play?"

"Not that I know. Aunt had asked me here to round out the table, so to speak, and, on the QT, watch for the Wentworth drama. She suspected Letty would make a scene. It was my job to minimize the damage. I thought I had when I separated the combatants after our dance, hoping everyone would think it was part of the evening's entertainment. I am wearing a red rose, but I really didn't have a part."

"Humph!" snorted Mrs. Browning. "Well, Letty's death will be part of the entertainment for the entire city. I will be the laughing-stock of Louisville. Murder under the stars, how appropriate."

"Mrs. Browning, pardon me," interjected Silky, "but I didn't know you were related. I read the society pages and have seen photographs of the two of you together, but the captions never read 'Paige and sister Letitia' or vice versa."

"We're stepsisters. My parents divorced because of her mother. My poor mother died an early death because of that woman. After that, I never wanted anything to do with my father. Letty appeared on the scene about five years ago. I guess we've had a quiet competition going ever since we discovered each other. I didn't really hate her; I just didn't like her or want to be around her."

"So why was she here tonight?" asked Bill.

"She bought a ticket! I couldn't very well refuse her. Letty was incensed over the breakup of her marriage. Robert was leaving her for his 'personal assistant,' a younger version of Letty. Turnabout is fair play. Robert was just doing to Letty what my father did to my mother. What a mess. What are we going to do, Richard?"

While Richard considered the matter, Artie turned to Bill and said, "We're going to call the police and let them sort this out. There must be a hundred people here tonight, if you count all the guests, serving staff, and musicians. All of us are suspects."

"No. Not all of us are," said Silky. "Most only had a passing acquaintance with Mrs. Wentworth. My vote for chief suspect is Robert and the unnamed trollop. I'd find out where they've been. And why Letty is in here, rather than out in the garden with the actors. Mrs. Browning, what part was she to play?"

"I was afraid you were going to ask. In a moment of childish pique, I asked that she be assigned the role of the victim. She was about to be poisoned tonight, only out at the table." Mrs. Browning glanced at her watch. "In about ten minutes."

Silky put her finger to her mouth and walked toward the body. "Why did she come into this room? Maybe her husband told her he wanted to talk to her. She came but didn't trust him. That's why she brought the gun. She thought he was going to do her harm. He knew about her part in the play and took this opportunity to rid himself of the old wife."

She began to pace, spinning her tale of how Robert lured Letty into the drawing room. Silky moved to the bar at the far end of the room. "Robert says, 'Let's have a drink for old times' sake,' and he mixed their drinks here. He adds the poison to hers and hands it to her. She tosses it back, ready to do battle. He watches her fall to the floor and departs, leaving the bottle of poison?" Silky pointed to the small bottle next to the decanter on the antique server doubling as the bar. "Here on the bar. Why would he do that?"

"Name your poison," said Richard, his first relevant uttering since finding his sister-in-law's body.

"What did you say?" Bill asked.

"Name your poison. That's what Robert always asked when he was bartending at his home. He's in pharmaceutical sales. Quite the success, by his account. Anyway, he had a hobby of collecting old bottles, the ones traveling salesmen used to peddle—the cure-all tonics. He also had several bottles plainly marked with the skull and crossbones. A lot of poisons used to be readily available. These old bottles were on the top shelf behind the bar. He would point to them and ask you to 'name your poison.' First-time guests always sputtered, and Robert got the biggest kick out of their reaction. And, if I'm not mistaken, that bottle is either one of his collection or made to look like one."

Richard had everyone's attention now. They walked over to the bottle and stared.

Silky bowed, saying, "There you have it."

Artie sat down, covering his face with his hands, shaking his head. The Brownings stood, holding hands, and looked at Silky, who was smiling broadly, very pleased with herself. Bill walked over to her and put his hands on her shoulders.

"Silky, this is no parlor game. You can't jump up and say that it was Robert Wentworth in the drawing room with a bottle of doctored bourbon. We need to call the police."

"We will. Just not at this moment. Are we missing anything else?" asked Silky, ignoring Bill.

"Just most of the facts, ma'am," said Artie. "Robert is not a stupid man. If he were going to kill Letty, he wouldn't poison her when everyone who knows him knows what Richard just told us."

"Nor would he leave the bottle behind," said Bill, shrugging at Silky's glare.

Artie said, "Letty was pretty drunk. You don't suppose she accidentally killed herself? Maybe there was some poison in the bottle and she didn't know it."

Mrs. Browning countered with, "It could have been suicide. I know she was depressed about the divorce. More than once she called me, crying that her life was over. More like her lifestyle. She probably decided to use my party to ruin both her husband and me. She kills herself but makes it look like Robert did it."

Just then the door opened and Robert Wentworth poked his head inside. "Oh, Paige, there you are. Have you seen Letty? Her big scene is coming up and she's gone missing. Everyone is looking for her. I thought I saw you heading this way with her a while ago."

Before Mrs. Browning could answer, another head appeared. It was Peter Hunt, the director for Murder on Call. "Is she here?" He turned to the young woman behind him who was the other half of the earlier altercation in the dance room. "If we can't find her, Maria, you'll just have to shoot someone else and we'll improvise a reason. I don't understand where Letty has gone."

"Shoot her?" asked Bill. "I thought Mrs. Wentworth was supposed to be poisoned."

"Oh, that was last month's script," replied Peter. "We've been working on changes these last few weeks. Letty and Robert had the best idea for a lovers' quarrel, more than the usual triangle." He turned to Maria. "We'd better get back before the whole play falls apart."

As Robert left, he turned back to Bill. "I need to see you later about playing next month for our anniversary party. Looking forward to another great show. Paige, this one is a doozy."

"Wait, Mr. Wentworth," called Bill. "I thought you and your wife were getting a divorce."

"Stuff and nonsense. Letty really gets into a part. Been spending the month convincing everyone I'm a cad and she is a wicked witch. She's having a ball. Gotta run." And he was off.

Bill looked at Artie, who looked at Mrs. Browning, who looked at her husband, who looked at Silky.

Silky walked over to look at Letitia Wentworth's body. Turning to the rest, she said, "So much for her moment in the spotlight. I guess we may have overlooked one important element."

"I'm afraid to ask, but I will," said Bill. "What did we overlook?"

"The play," replied Silky. "What if someone really wanted to kill another person? What better way than to use the play as cover? If the victim was to be poisoned, why not use that as my method to kill the person I wanted out of the way? That way, the death could be misconstrued as an accident or, as Mrs. Browning said, suicide."

"But Letitia was to be shot, not poisoned, if we can believe Robert and Peter," said Artie. "That negates Letty's death as an accident or suicide, at least for me."

Bill walked toward the door. "I hate to bring this up again, but it's past time to call the police. At this rate, we all will have plenty of time to solve the crime. I'm sure the cops will be happy to assign adjoining cells."

Silky went to Mrs. Browning's side. "They'll only need one cell, won't they, Mrs. Browning? You didn't know about the change in the script, but you knew about the poison collection. Mrs. Wentworth wouldn't refuse to celebrate the evening with just one more mint julep. You made sure it was her last mint julep. I'd say 'Nuts to you,' but that reminds me of almonds. Let's go, Bill. You didn't happen to get payment in advance, did you?"

Bill opened the door to let Silky pass.

She turned to Artie and said, "We'll make that call now. Well,

Deputy Sheriff Goodman, I guess you'd better stay with your aunt."

With that she sailed out of the room.

Artie leaned against the doorjamb and watched them depart. "Say good night, Silky."

But she didn't.

The Ohio River, 981 miles long, is the largest tributary of the Mississippi River. It has provided the means to move goods up and down from Pittsburgh, Pennsylvania, to St. Louis, Missouri. At the point on the river where Louisville sits today, a twenty-six-foot drop over two and a half miles marks the Falls of the Ohio. In the 18th and 19th centuries, all boats had to be off-loaded at Louisville and transported over land up or downriver. A canal and set of locks were later built to facilitate shipping.

Today the riverfront holds a variety of parks, restaurants, and sports facilities. Two weeks before the Derby, a great fireworks celebration takes places over the Ohio River. With all the crowds and noise, the riverfront becomes a perfect setting for murder.

RIVER BLUFF

by Sandra Cerow Leonard

Sandra Cerow Leonard has the passion of a convert for Kentucky life and history, having grown up in New England and lived in Southern California for almost thirty years. All of her previous writing was related to her employment and included bureaucratic pontificating as a public-sector administrator, and circuitous arguments and clarifications as an attorney. She presently lives near Louisville with her husband, son, granddaughter Megan, five cats, and a canine cotton ball named Buster.

"TO SUCCESS." Missy raised her mint julep, the drink of the Kentucky Derby, saluting the white blooms in the dogwood trees just off the end of the terrace. This year's spring wind and rain were gentle. Most of the blossoms still decorated the branches of the trees; there had been no dogwood winter, no cold snap where petals fall like soft snow, coating the ground and baring leafless twigs. The large, old trees glowed in the morning light. "To Kentucky's first Saturday in May."

Glimmers of the mighty Ohio River radiated through the bushes, shrubs, and trees of the magnificent natural garden before her. She loved the spring flowers blooming on the edge of one of the many sinkholes topping the limestone caverns that riddled the area. For almost one hundred years, people had admired the grounds of the stone mansion on the river bluff in Louisville. The garden was, at least partially, designed by Frederick Law Olmsted, whose landscape firm created New York City's Central Park, the Capitol grounds in Washington, D.C., as well as Iroquois, Shawnee, and Cherokee Parks in Louisville. Olmsted loved sinkholes, leaving them in the gardens he planned in Kentucky to accentuate the natural contours of the landscape.

Missy had done her homework, as usual. She knew a whole lot about the old mansion, the scandals and finances of its parade of owners and inhabitants, the history of the gardens, and, even, the sinkholes. Aloud, she said, "I've come a long way from the streets and the smells of Butchertown where I played as a kid." Her father had worked in the stockyards and had come home at night smelling of the slaughter.

There was a soft click behind her. "Yes, Missy, you have. We both have."

Missy's hand came down violently, spilling a little of the bourbon drink on the gray stone slabs of the terrace. "I didn't hear you open the French doors, Jack. You were busy talking to the governor a few minutes ago. It looked like a serious conversation."

"It was nice of him to show up. He's very interested," Jack said.

She nodded. "It's a big day for us, and it took a long time to get here, but I can't help thinking, Lou and CeCe might have enjoyed being at this party. After all, it's only been a few years since they disappeared." The soft Southern notes in her voice were faint, having been sharpened in the years before the Bar Association and the innumerable conferences with the gray-suited, silver-haired white males who were the power establishment in town.

"Yes, Missy, Lou would have liked being here. But not for the same reasons as you and me. Lou liked power. At one time, he would have enjoyed having brunch with all the politically and financially important folks here. When we became partners in our own law firm, he was quick to tell me that he was on a short track to governor of Kentucky. The group at this brunch could certainly help that dream come true."

"You're right," Missy agreed. "CeCe, on the other hand, was a butterfly. Folks enjoyed looking at her and didn't mind that her attention span was notoriously short." A balmy breeze sent the fresh scent of warm spring sun on new-mown grass into the air around them. "You and I, however . . . we've finally made it up the river bluffs to a Glenview Kentucky Derby brunch."

Jack smiled at her but didn't say anything. He had been Lou's partner for years, but Missy had always felt a little awkward around Jack because he'd known her too long and too well. Their parents had been friends, and they had grown up in the same classes in the same schools, even going to their senior prom together.

Jack and Missy both looked off the terrace to the river, silently wrapped in their own thoughts.

Missy wasn't her real name, it was Michelle, just like the old Beatles song. But as a teenager she'd learned that the girls in Louisville's best circles dressed in preppy clothes, went to Collegiate School, and were named Cissy, MeMe, Weezie, Booper, Muffy, and KiKi. She changed her name, spent some of her waitressing earnings on crew-neck sweaters and button-down shirts, but she had to wait until college to go to the right school—on a scholarship, of course. Her grades were outstanding, and she even managed law school before coming back home to Louisville to a prestigious law firm as its single, token female attorney.

From the perspective of the law firm partners, their exercise in affirmative action went well. The pompous and pin-striped liked her work, but in a city that prized women for their decorative beauty and docile personalities, she'd have to wait a long time to make partner herself.

The work they gave her was not a fast track to the top of the Louisville legal heap; it was the partners' idea of suitable for a Southern lady lawyer, a lot of document drafting and court appearances for scheduling continuances and uncontested hearings. No litigation, no arguments, no hostile negotiations.

She'd met Lou at the firm. As soon as she was introduced to the golden boy from the well-known family, she intended to marry him. He'd had the childhood she always wanted, and everything he wanted came easily to him, including Missy's heart. She saw to that. But what she couldn't see was that he would become such a liability to the future she planned for herself. Although, if she was being honest, she had to give him credit—he played the stereotypical games of a successful life very well.

Jack came into the firm a year later. He'd married CeCe right out of law school, and her father's connections got him the job at the firm. While very different in almost all aspects, Jack and Lou became fast friends. Both worked hard and, like the partners, filed numerous motions with the courts requiring their personal appearances, generated mountains of paperwork, and billed their clients for every possible activity, including morning coffee conferences with each other. *Conference with colleague, re: Sheldon matter—15 minutes.* Those conferences billed at the firm's hourly rate for an attorney really added up in a year.

From childhood, Lou had been programmed to be ambitious. For several years, he worked at least the 2040 billable hours required each year of a young attorney in the firm. When he decided he wanted a political career, he convinced Jack to move out of the firm with him to form their own legal corporation, being very careful to get the partners' support first.

The partners, anticipating success for the young men in coming years, envisioned basking in reflected power of knowing yet another future governor of the state. Power by association. Meanwhile, they did not have to share any of the firm's day-to-day financial assets with Jack or Lou to help achieve that goal.

The tinkle of glassware and the soft music of a string quartet wafted over the sunlit terrace. Missy grimaced as she sipped from the year's special Derby glass. "Bourbon isn't my drink, but that's a sacrilege at a Derby brunch party. I like the taste of the mint, though."

Jack grinned at her and gazed back over the garden, his garden.

Instead of continuing as the token female in the firm, doing the legal work the partners deigned to give her, Missy said very nice farewells to them, ran for Circuit Court, and won her first judgeship. Of course, it helped that the incumbent had some serious skeletons in his closet. Someone had anonymously told the *Courier-Journal* about the judge's peccadilloes; it published an exposé, and the voters resoundingly indicated they were ready for a change. Missy donned the black robes and went on the bench, making sure that she was well liked by the attorneys who practiced in her court. She was active in the local Bar Association, had the Association endorsement, and continued to be reelected with ease.

"Don't you think we should go back to the party, Missy?"

"Just a few more minutes. Let the governor talk to some of our guests."

Everything had gone well for all of them, until Lou came home one night and told her that he thought it was time to run for his first elected office. She had known it was going to happen but not what came next. "Missy, I think you should resign from the bench so you can devote all of your time to being the wife of the next state representative from our part of Jefferson County. It wouldn't do to have one of your court decisions become controversial and get used as campaign fodder by the opposition. Having you smiling by my side could make all the difference."

How could someone be married for as long as they had been and not have a clue what made the other person tick? Missy had worked long and hard to get where she was and had many future plans for herself. The plans did not include being just a smiling arm adornment for an aspiring politician. She initially put Lou off;

she had several important cases coming up—long, complicated ones—and it would be unfair to try to seat another judge for them. That worked for several months, but Lou became increasingly insistent. Since her plans did not include a divorce, she knew she had to do something, fast.

It took a while for Missy to arrange, but CeCe and Lou began an affair. Missy had orchestrated numerous social occasions that thrust them together. She would often beg out at the last minute, citing her court workload. Lou and CeCe were both beautiful, self-indulgent people from the same background; the affair was bound to happen.

Jack wasn't around much either, because he'd had to take up the slack at their successful law office, now that Lou was campaigning. Missy didn't know when Jack found out about the affair, but he did, and he didn't seem to mind. Maybe affairs were part of being married to CeCe; maybe he wanted some hold over Lou for the future.

Lou and CeCe were discreet. They spent a lot of time at the dock where Lou's small boat was anchored. At that time of year, not many people were around.

The spring weather had been turbulent—snow, torrential rain, and tornadoes. The mud-brown Ohio was full of debris; whole trees bounced along on the swift current. In low-lying areas, the floodplain was underwater.

Louisville had been settled on the upper end of the falls of the Ohio River because they had been the only obstacle to navigation on the long river. Before the dam and locks were built, the rough water fell twenty-four feet over a two-mile course. Below the falls of the Ohio, a huge pile of detritus, several miles long, accumulated, since everything that passed down the river ended its journey by crashing at the foot of the cascade.

Missy had noticed the immense, tangled heap on her way back to Louisville from a meeting in New Albany, Indiana. In the mess, there were several small boats, a large wooden chest, and something big and white, possibly a refrigerator.

She stopped in a parking lot on the riverbank to collect her thoughts before going on to her next meeting. Pyrotechnicians were wiring some of the explosives to the Clark Memorial Bridge for the country's largest fireworks show, Thunder Over Louisville, scheduled for the next Saturday. Lou had mentioned that he thought that they should go to the display with Jack and CeCe and watch from the boat, starting early to see the spectacular six-hour air show that preceded the fireworks.

Later that same night, Lou went into Missy's home office next to the den. He looked tense, twisting his hands as he spoke. He told her he'd spent a lot of time thinking in the past few months. The life track he had been on just didn't satisfy him anymore. He wanted to stop and smell the roses. CeCe and he loved each other and they wanted to leave Kentucky to create a life together that was fun, not heavy with duty and responsibility. He said CeCe was talking to Jack at the same time.

Missy was stunned. What a change in attitude from the months when he had started his political campaign, even from the years when she had first met him. For once she had been seriously wrong. "I don't know what to say, Lou. I have a Bar meeting tonight. Let me think about this, and we can talk about it again tomorrow."

She was so taut that she barely saw River Road as she drove downtown to the meeting. A divorce, which could prove publicly nasty since they were now public figures, was out of the question. As usual, she considered solutions that would most benefit her. One obvious problem was, whose income would Lou and CeCe live on?

Dividing the assets Lou and Missy owned or trying to divide the law firm was out of the question. All four of them would end up broke. Missy had worked too long to agree to anything that would require her to start over again, and Jack would feel the same way.

Though Lou and CeCe both came from families with money, they had not inherited much. But getting rid of Lou and CeCe would help Missy with her personal goals if it was done carefully. In fact, she couldn't wait to get rid of them—for good.

The planning began in earnest. She knew that the law firm had multimillion-dollar key-man life insurance. She'd had a court case recently, which revolved around a key-man policy, and she'd learned all the intricacies of the insurance. If Lou died, the firm would be paid millions from the policy to help make up for the loss of one of the two partners. But Jack was already working hard to make up for the absence of the other partner. The firm didn't really need all the money to make up for the loss of Lou. Missy, using her cell phone, made an appointment to talk to Jack.

Where would you put two bodies into the Ohio River where they would be presumed dead but probably never be found? Missy couldn't risk having anyone think Lou and CeCe's deaths were anything but a stupid accident.

She knew the river well. Her father's favorite relaxation was to take his ancient, small boat onto the river in the summer evenings to fish. The dumpy boat on a little trailer off the back alley was hitched to the old car after supper. Dad and Missy drove to one of the free public boat ramps near whatever spot he thought fish might be biting that week. They'd fish until it was almost dark and then drive home, where her mother would be sitting on the little front porch, waiting for them, after finishing the dishes. Anything they caught would be breaded and fried for dinner the next day.

Where would her father dump something he didn't ever want found? After careful consideration Missy was sure he'd select the George Rogers Clark Homesite in Clarksville, Indiana.

* * *

On the way to Indiana, the Ohio waters thundering over the dam were the color of a Starbucks latte. Huge logs crashed as they hit the rocks under the falls, splintering into smaller water-logged pieces. Below the falls, ten-foot-high piles of debris lined the Indiana side of the river. Lou's small boat, tied to some of the wreckage at the foot of the ribbed concrete boat ramp, bobbed precariously in the rushing waters.

In the summer, the river was placid below the 19th-century log cabin, which represented the home of George Rogers Clark, a founder of Louisville and older brother to William Clark of the famed Lewis and Clark expedition. Numerous fishermen flicked their bait into the blue water. But spring, especially this spring, was a different story. The river pounded over the falls of the Ohio into a living, throbbing, blood-stopping pulse.

A foggy mist wound around the trees on the riverbank as CeCe and Lou jumped out of her Mercedes and ran toward Missy. "I'm scared," CeCe said. "It's so loud, and the river looks so powerful. Lou tied the raveled rope you gave us to the post in the water up there on the Indiana bank way above the falls. It's so early in the morning that no one saw us drive to the old broken pier and leave Lou's car, and no one saw us leave either."

It was so simple. Sometime soon, the empty boat would be found severely damaged below the falls. Lou and CeCe would have been reported missing. An investigation would reveal only that they had left together early for the boat to load the food and drinks, waiting for Jack and Missy to join them for a day on the river watching the air show and Thunder Over Louisville.

Jack and Missy had an early morning meeting with a governor's representative who was in Louisville for the festivities. He had assured them that the meeting would not take long; he just wanted to discuss his pet project, a new computer setup in the Circuit Court, from the perspective of a judge and an attorney. The local Bar Association, at almost no discernible prodding from

Missy, had recommended Missy and Jack. No one else wanted to work on a day of Derby Festival play and fun.

The scheduling of the meeting was fortuitous. Missy and Jack had an unimpeachable alibi for when the accident was supposed to have occurred. They dressed casually for the computer meeting. They would not have time to go home to change, so they had to be careful not to get their clothing wet or dirty on the boat ramp in the early morning mist.

"Are you sure this is the only way?" CeCe wailed.

Since they wouldn't be found, Lou and CeCe would be presumed to have died when the boat broke loose from its moorings and hurtled over the falls. The question that would be asked was, why hadn't they started the boat engine and just motored safely to the river bank? A careful examination of what was left of the boat engine would show a screw had come loose and fallen into the bilges where the dark oily water completely concealed the errant fastener.

"I'm sure," Missy said, determinedly. "Let me help you in. Lou is already on the boat stowing some of the food. Do you have the drinks? It's almost sunrise."

CeCe handed her a bag, and the three of them walked down the ramp. Lou took a bag from Jack and disappeared inside. He came back out and took the other bags. "Thanks for everything. We owe you both more than we can ever repay."

You have no idea what you owe us, Missy thought maliciously.

Jack shook Lou's hand, took the keys to CeCe's car from her, and gave her a kiss on the cheek. "I hope your new life is all you want it to be."

He went back up the ramp to quickly drive the Mercedes home and pick up his own car, since he had to make an appearance at a breakfast meeting before showing up at the computer meeting. They all watched him drive off and knew it was the end of their lives together.

Missy picked up the heavy wooden oar from the side of the boat. It was used to push the boat off the shore, not to paddle the boat. Lou popped out of the boat door and bent to open the access in the side rail as he helped CeCe lift the cooler of drinks onto the deck. Missy felt the oar's heft in her hands. She thought of all she still wanted to accomplish in her life. She thought of Lou and CeCe, not understanding how they could want to leave all they had, so much more than what she and Jack had started with.

It was so easy. Smash! A couple of cracks as they crouched over the cooler, knock them overboard, and the mad river would rush them irretrievably downstream to bash against the bridges, if they didn't drown first. Missy just wanted to finish it. She was very tired of all the plotting and scheming.

Everything went as planned. Missy loosened the boat and pushed it from shore, taking all of the strength she had left. The boat collided with a log as it jumped over a wave, and she could see one of the food bags fall into the roaring water. As the boat crashed downstream, the garbage in the water smashed into it as it made its way inexorably toward the massive stone column of the downstream bridge.

The computer meeting in Jack's law office was not the short encounter promised, because it was the representative's pet project. Missy and Jack had used the program extensively, were very knowledgeable about it, and had a number of recommendations for improving the software. The representative apologized for keeping them, hoping they would not mind missing much of the air exhibition but hoping they would enjoy Thunder. There were more than 50,000 fireworks in this year's show, he'd heard.

Jack and Missy finally left in her car from the garage under the office. Because of the bridge and street closures for Thunder, they slowly made their roundabout way to the Indiana shore. The fireworks would be on the ground, on the bridge over the Ohio, and on two large barges in the river. They made it to the other side of the river by dusk, just an hour before the fireworks, and pulled up to the broken pier.

Many other boats with inhabitants who had been partying all day were in the area. They waved and chatted with a few of the boaters they knew. The raveled rope hung to the broken pier, and no one thought much of it until Jack and Missy asked everyone around if they had seen Lou's boat. No one had, but one of the boaters finally surmised through an alcoholic daze that a boating accident might have occurred and called the Coast Guard.

The boat eventually was found twenty miles downstream, and there was, subsequently, a finding that CeCe and Lou had died in a boating accident. Months later, the insurance company paid the face amount of the policy. Jack and Missy went to dinner to celebrate.

"How sad they are," everyone said. When they started to go to parties together, everyone said, "How nice for them." When they married, everyone was invited and said, "They deserve some happiness."

When they bought the limestone mansion on the bluff, everyone said, "That's what happens when you work hard." When they decided to give their first Derby brunch, they invited everyone, even the governor, who gladly accepted the invitation.

Missy turned and smiled, putting her hand through Jack's arm. "Let's go back to our guests."

As they entered the room, the governor, holding his mint julep, came up to them. "I meant what I asked you on the phone last night, Missy. I want you to run for lieutenant governor in the next election." He raised his glass to her. "To success."

The Kentucky bourbon swirled around in the raised glass. The Mexican Riviera was exquisite; the azure sea, rippling from a gentle breeze, sparkled in the sinking sun. The tanned couple smiled fondly at each other as they toasted the glorious sunset.

"What a life," he said. "I really could do this forever."

"That's good," she replied, "because we can't ever go back. And the boat you just bought cost a lot of what money we have left. But the boat is really beautiful, and everyone is going to want to go fishing on it."

"I hope so. Thank goodness the key-man insurance finally paid off. It took long enough. I'm going to start advertising our new fishing service tomorrow. When Missy drove us to the Cincinnati airport on Thunder morning with our clothes, tickets, and false passports, we couldn't have predicted it would take a couple of years for the final payout. Good thing you and I had been stashing money away for six months before we decided to talk to Missy and Jack."

"It's also a good thing that Missy and Jack were honest enough to send us our half of the money to the offshore bank account. Who would have thought you and I would end up a pair of happy beach bums and Missy and Jack would take our places on the river bluff?"

Lou raised his glass to CeCe. "To success."

The Kentucky Derby is not just a race, it's the cornerstone for a great number of parties, parades, silly races, and a variety of entertainment.

As the popularity of the Derby grew, so did a burgeoning industry, one catering to hometown folks and tourists alike. Every day now, for two weeks leading up to the first Saturday in May, everyone can enjoy some event.

On the Thursday before the Derby, the Pegasus Parade is held. It has evolved from a few marching bands and decorated cars to a small version of the Macy's Thanksgiving Day parade. All Kentuckians watch on TV. Competition runs high to be the "Best." Reputations are on the line.

How far would you go to win? Would murder be in your plans?

The Squirrel Is Falling
by Tamera Huber

—✦—

Tamera Huber is a writer of fiction and nonfiction, concentrating on screenplays and short stories. Her feature articles appear in many regional publications. Most recently, she completed her first mystery novel.

"I'll kill him!"

Margo Wells paced up and down Baxter Avenue on the late-April day, waiting for word. The blue, 60-degree skies were preferable to the near freezing temperatures that began Derby Week.

Problems for Margo's troupe of weary balloon handlers had persisted throughout the day, beginning with a thrown rod in the lead parade vehicle that had backed up traffic for miles. With fifteen minutes before the scheduled start of the annual Pegasus Parade, their lead balloon handler was missing. Kevin Kaplan had been at the strategy session the preceding night but had not shown up for the early-morning calisthenics that Margo had forced her team to endure each morning for the previous three months.

Jamie Denton, a petite woman in a purple polo shirt and jeans, stopped and reported to her similarly clad boss. "I . . . can't . . . find. . . ," Jamie gasped.

"Spit it out!" Margo ordered.

"Him . . . anywhere," Jamie answered, then bent down to touch her knees and suck in air.

"Larry!" Margo screamed.

He was there in a flash, also sporting a purple polo and jeans. "Yes, Ms. Wells?"

"Are you sure you saw Kevin?" she asked.

"About ten minutes ago," he replied. "He was buying one of those blow-up aliens. Over there." The junior manager and right ballast pointed toward the plastic paraphernalia vendor stationed at the corner of Broadway and Baxter, the beginning of the Pegasus Parade route.

Margo glared down at Jamie.

"I . . . already . . . asked. . . . The guy . . . didn't . . . see. . . ." Margo's assistant took a full gulp of air and added, "Where Kevin . . . went," before she collapsed to the pavement.

This was Margo's big chance. The balloon sponsored by First Trust Bank had won a coveted early spot in the procession. The three-story-tall Spider-Man had risen from last year's sixteenth to this year's second slot, surpassing Lisa St. Claire's Rocky the Flying Squirrel by three places.

Margo wouldn't allow the opportunity to gloat pass. Each year, she and St. Claire, her rival from United Farmer's Bank, vied for position and performance in the parade. As a hedge against losing face, Margo had hired a ringer. But Kevin, the Macy's Parade veteran who netted $60,000 as a mail clerk, had disappeared.

Strains of "When the Saints Go Marching In" wafted from two slots up. The Grand National Champions, the Truman High Marching Wolverines, were a perfect choice to begin the parade. Their red-and-gold uniforms gleamed in the sun. Two lovely young women who held the Pegasus Parade banner preceded the band.

"Jamie! Larry!" Margo shouted.

"Right here," Jamie said, as Larry helped her out of the gutter.

"Larry, you're filling in for Kevin."

He nodded and looked as if he'd been punched in his stomach. "And Jamie, you're filling in for me."

"I'm what?" she asked, but the exhausted assistant didn't have the strength to argue. "Yes, ma'am," Jamie answered by rote.

"I'm going to look for him myself," Margo said, taking off in the direction of the corn-dog stand. She maneuvered her way around big-footed clowns, horse piles, and sticky children with cotton-candy hair. No Kevin. After staring at the plastic aliens and glow wands for several minutes, Margo formulated a plan.

Unencumbered due to her parade credentials in her role as vice president, she entered the procession from the sidelines, slipping quietly behind Jamie, who had recovered enough to lead the First Trust contingent. The young woman jumped a foot when the VP whispered in her ear, "Get them to clamp down on the ropes! Control, Jamie, control!"

Margo moved deliberately, slowly enough for each advancing group to overtake her. The Grand Marshal, Zeke Mayborn, the new conference-winning football coach for River City University, waved from a red convertible. When the sports car caught up to Margo, she couldn't resist the opportunity to ask Mayborn for a signed football as a donation for her company's upcoming United for the Arts campaign, offering her phone number and a wink to the very-married coach. Lisa St. Claire's card was already in his breast pocket.

A group of beautifully brushed and tasseled Arabian horses pranced in unison behind the coach's entourage. Margo continued her slow-motion pace. Lisa's balloon volunteers approached as Margo sidestepped the treasures left behind by the equestrians.

The First Trust VP blended into the left flank of her rival's contingent. There, in the lead position, was Kevin. *Her* ringer. *Her* employee. Lisa was right by his side, smiling broadly, holding a plastic alien and looking at Kevin's deep, dark muscles.

After the balloon handlers performed the necessary maneu-
vers to avoid a collision with the I-65 overpass, Margo moved
quickly in front of Kevin, then stopped. She bent down, pretending to tie her shoe.

Although Kevin had brawn and experience, he did not possess
light feet. Before Lisa could steady him, the outrageously paid
mail clerk fell over Margo's back. As he tumbled on top of his
soon-to-be ex-boss, the muscle-bound man released his hold on
the rope attached to Rocky's left foot.

In a chain reaction worthy of the highest award at a dominoes
competition or a Marx Brothers movie, each of the subsequent
handlers tripped or fell behind Margo and Kevin, releasing their
grips on the ropes that had kept the squirrel earthbound.

After Margo and Lisa extricated themselves from the human
pile, Lisa took the first swing. She missed, but the unfortunate
street entertainer who had come over to help the handlers to their
feet went down hard. The honks in Morse code emanating from
the clown's spiral horn signaled for help and ricocheted off the
concrete overpass.

Like sumo wrestlers, Margo and Lisa dove at one another. Lisa
lost her balance first, and the pair landed with a thud onto Broadway's pavement. On their way down, they knocked over parade-
goers and security personnel who had come to help.

What originally began as a rescue effort quickly turned into a
melee. In the midst of the brawl, the mingled and mangled colors included dark blue police uniforms; red clown noses and feet;
purple, orange, and gold band uniforms; white majorette hats;
brown sheriff outfits; and all shades of horseflesh.

When Margo and Lisa staggered to their feet, they saw Rocky
floating north toward the Ohio River. Lisa chased after it but
tripped and fell face-first into a cotton-candy stand. The wind
picked up, moving the balloon higher out of reach.

Within seconds, an alert, if not overzealous, parade security guard called the Kentucky Air National Guard, four miles away.

Alarms sounded. A few minutes later, an F-16 scrambled from the tarmac. The jet caught up to and circled the wayward squirrel, who represented an imminent threat to Hoosier homeland security.

"Are we go for launch?" Echo One asked.

"That's affirmative," said ground commander Tucker.

"Are you sure this one's a bogie?" asked the pilot.

"Affirmative. Collateral damage must be avoided—at all costs," the commander emphasized.

"Target acquired. Fire one."

Upon impact, the gas-filled cartoon character blew apart, raining chunks of rubberized squirrel parts into the muddy, churning river. Coast Guard and Louisville Police water patrols stopped traffic at the Kennedy Bridge to avoid civilian casualties and, more importantly, to discourage souvenir seekers.

Commander Tucker watched the radar from the Air Guard's situation room as the large, odd-shaped blip on the screen dissolved. The room erupted with a collective *Hoo-ya*.

"Target down over the Ohio," said Echo One. "I repeat, Squirrel is in the Big Muddy. No damage. Joe's Crab Shack unaffected. I repeat, dinner still on for tonight."

"Good work, Captain. Return to base," Tucker said.

At the corner of Broadway and Floyd, Margo and Lisa watched the destruction against the otherwise calm Indiana skyline. They sat on empty bleacher seats. A giant, rubber eyeball floated south past a flock of geese headed north, and fell into the waiting Ohio.

"Better luck next year," Margo said as she patted Lisa's back.

"It's your turn, you know," replied her rival.

Margo nodded. "I'll dump him in the landfill. Like the others."

"That drum worked really well last year. Don't forget the lime," said Lisa.

As the pair rose, Lisa said, "Same time next year?"

"Wouldn't miss it."

The perfect racehorse has been the subject of debate among breeders, trainers, jockeys, and racing aficionados since the sport began. War Admiral vs. Whirlaway; Man o' War vs. Northern Dancer. The speed, stamina, and especially the heart of the horse are the ingredients needed for a champion.

One issue not up for debate is that the Kentucky Derby tests any pretender to the "perfect horse" title. Only one horse, Secretariat, has broken "the greatest two minutes in sports," reducing it to 1:59.2.

Was he the perfect horse or simply the best? The search continues.

ANONYMOUS
by Brenda Stewart

Brenda Robertson Stewart has a degree in English from Indiana University. She is a painter, sculptor, and forensic artist who reconstructs skulls for identification purposes. For twenty years she was a professional doll artist specializing in Native American sculptures. A horse breeder for many years, she raised Tennessee Walking Horses and racing quarter horses. A mystery buff since a child, Brenda completed her first mystery novel in 2002. The manuscript, a finalist in the St. Martin's/Malice Domestic Contest in 2003, is currently being circulated to publishers. "Anonymous" is her first published short story. She grew up in southern Indiana and currently resides near Indianapolis.

DIRK CARTER SNEAKED toward the "put together" fence. He was determined to look through a crack to see what was happening on the other side. Hearing thundering hooves, he knew a horse ran somewhere near. Just as he was about to step up to the fence, he heard a low growl to his right.

He turned to see the biggest and ugliest mongrel dog that had ever graced the planet. Backing away from the fence, with his eyes glued to the beast moving toward him, he turned quickly and ran toward his pickup truck parked beside the road. The dog, in turn, ran after the fleeing man.

Dirk almost made it to the vehicle, but the hairy critter lunged forward, grabbing his leg. The flesh tore, and the bottom of the denim pant leg was ripped completely from Dirk's body. Fumbling with the truck door, the panting man opened it and threw himself onto the seat, slamming the door behind him. The dog was distracted for a moment by the cloth hanging from his teeth, but he tore it away with his paw and attacked the door, leaving long scratches down the side.

The engine fired, and Dirk floored the accelerator, spewing dirt and gravel all over the animal, but it didn't deter the avenger one bit. Out of the corner of his eye, Dirk saw someone dart out from behind the fence as the dog bounced away from the speeding vehicle. Recovering quickly, the monster chased the truck and almost caught it at one point, before finally giving up.

Blood trickled down Dirk's leg, but he didn't stop until he crossed the river into Louisville, cursing all the way. He was staying at a fleabag motel because he didn't want to attract attention to himself. He pulled into the space in front of his room, and when he was reasonably certain he didn't have an audience, he limped inside.

Looking down at his leg, he realized the dog had bit into it. It was bleeding like a son of a bitch. He grabbed a towel and soaked it in cold water, then applied it to his wound. It stung like fire. He wanted some ice but was afraid he would be seen going to the ice machine.

He hoped he didn't need any stitches. Last time he went to one of those immediate care centers, the nurse seemed real suspicious when he explained how he had been hurt. *Wasn't none of her damned business,* he thought.

Dirk Carter wasn't even his real name, but all his IDs were in that name for this trip. Sometimes, he couldn't even remember his real name.

He worked for a consortium in southern California, but he had grown up down by the Ohio River in southern Indiana. Every fall he had to travel around the country, searching for that elusive colt that could win the Kentucky Derby for his bosses. It wasn't the money that interested them, but the glory of owning the winning colt. They wanted to be interviewed on TV so all their friends could see them. If they could win the Triple Crown, the group told Dirk they would pay him a million-dollar bonus.

This trip had not been lucrative. He had found only one worthy colt, and that farmer down in Arkansas had wanted a king's ransom for his horse. Everyone wanted to get rich. Never mind that someone else had to get the colt in shape and train it.

And now here Dirk was, back at his old stomping ground. He had watched Solomon Miller's place every year, because the old goat knew his Thoroughbreds. More than once, he had sold some fast horses that had gone on the track. None had won the Derby, but several had done well at Santa Anita, where Dirk hung out when he wasn't working.

Even when Dirk was a boy, the man had been known as "Old Solomon." He was a strange bird who never uttered a sound if he didn't have to. It probably would not be wise to confront the old geezer.

Dirk had to find some way to silence that menacing mongrel and look behind the fence. He wondered when Solomon had gotten that dog anyway. He decided he'd go to the Red Dog Saloon that night to pick up any rumors about what the old fart might be hiding.

After Dirk's bleeding finally stopped, he made a makeshift bandage with a dry towel and then wrapped the entire lower leg with an Ace bandage that he always carried in his tack box. He lay back on his bed and tried to figure out how to get around that big mutt.

Maybe if he took meat he could hold the dog off long enough to get a look through a crack in the fence. Built with odd boards and pieces of whatever the builder could find, the fence might blow over if a good wind came up.

Poison was not an option. As much as he hated that monster, he couldn't bring himself to kill an animal. After all, animals had been his only real friends when he was a boy.

He tried to forget his childhood poverty and the abuse his family suffered at the hands of an alcoholic father. The more his dad drank, the meaner the man got. Dirk couldn't count the number of times he had been beaten trying to protect his mother and sister. Thank God, they were both gone now. He picked up the Western novel he'd been reading; it was going to be a long day.

About four that afternoon, the cowboy got up and examined his leg. It didn't hurt too much now. Putting on a fresh pair of jeans, he looked in the mirror and decided to shave. Taking the time to lather up his face, he slowly stroked the old safety razor over the lines and wrinkles, trying not to make any new nicks.

It didn't seem so long ago that he was a handsome young man with dark curly hair and smooth, tanned skin. The women had been wild for him. Here he was, middle-aged, but looking as old as Solomon Miller. He guessed that all those years he spent wrangling cattle out on the plains had weathered his skin to parchment, but when he looked into his own dark eyes, he could still see an unfulfilled yearning. He had spent his life as a drifter, going from one ranch to another, but he knew his horses. That's why the consortium had hired him to find good racehorses. *Guess I'm worth something,* he thought.

After grabbing some sandwiches at McDonald's, he drove east, wandering the back roads until he finally came to the Miller place by a roundabout way. The large gray dog was asleep on the porch of the small, nondescript farmhouse. Dirk couldn't remember the house when it hadn't needed painting. It had always been gray and dingy with shutters hanging at odd angles. It looked like someone had abandoned it many years ago. The lawn held dandelions, ragweeds, and what looked like Queen Anne's lace. There was a worn path where apparently the dog and old man walked to the rusty mailbox that hung on the post with a piece of wire wrapped around it.

Dirk passed the house and turned around in a wide spot where the weeds had been mashed down by farm equipment. When he drove back by the house, the gigantic mutt was standing up, staring toward the road. He could swear the dog recognized his truck, so he hurried on, wiping the sweat off his brow with his hand as he drove.

Heading south, Dirk didn't even look at the beautiful colors that painted the hills, or see the silver stream of water cascading over the cliffs. His mind was down by the river fifty years ago. He could see the little shanty he called home. It was surrounded by dirt, spread there by the river, which had overflowed its banks almost every spring. Built on stilts to keep it above the flood stage, many nights Dirk could hear the insistent water lapping at his bedroom floor. He had no fondness for water, whether it was in a river, the ocean, or a glass. Driving down the dirt road that ran along the banks of the Ohio, no shanties remained. His childhood had been washed away.

Darkness was creeping in as Dirk headed the dirty black truck toward the Red Dog Saloon. The parking lot was lined with pick-ups, as he knew it would be on Friday night. Pushing his Stetson on his head, he sauntered into the bar. A country band cranked out "Rocky Top" while the singer shook her booty in time to the music.

She looks a little like Lily, Dirk thought. He couldn't quite remember where he had known her, but he could remember what a sweet feeling it was to lay his head between her breasts.

A young fellow drank beer at the bar. He was small and wiry like a jockey. Dirk, ordering bourbon with two drops of water as usual, worked himself into hearing distance of the young drinker.

"What you and Old Solomon up to, Jimmy?" he heard someone ask the young man.

"Oh, not much, Brad. He's always got some colt he thinks can win the Derby. This year's is good, though. Probably the best I've ever rode. Old Solomon wants to train him a little more and then sell shares. Says he'll give me 20% and keep 40% for himself. Don't know if he'll ever find anyone to buy the rest of the shares; he's never done anything like this before. Still haven't taken the colt the distance, though. Want his bones to develop a little more. Don't want no splints on this colt."

The man named Brad said, "Where does he find those colts anyway? And where does he get the money to buy them? Have to cost a pretty penny."

Jimmy said, "That's something I can't tell you, 'cause I don't know. Every winter he takes his old truck and run-down trailer and is gone about two weeks. When he comes home, he always has a colt. Sometimes they're awfully sorry looking when he brings them in. He's had some good ones he's sold, though, so he has that money. Don't know about any pensions or such. Course, he inherited the farm from his folks. Maybe they left him some money too. He don't spend much either. Got all these old remedies for the colts and hisself. Spends more on that old dog he got than on anything else."

"Man, I saw that brute," said Brad. "Sure wouldn't want to tangle with him."

"You got that right," said Jimmy. "He's as big as a small pony. Someone was sneaking around this morning when I was riding. Ol' Fuzzy got him, though. Had some of his jeans leg, and there was blood on it too. Imagine, naming a creature like that 'Fuzzy.'"

Brad said, "How do you get along with that dog?"

"I don't turn my back on him. We get along okay."

"Where'd he get that dog anyway?"

"Beats me. Brought him back with the colt. Horse has a fit if Fuzzy isn't there. I think they sleep together."

Brad said, "Ain't that something? I've heard of some of those temperamental colts having cats, chickens, even goats as stablemates. Don't know how they keep from getting stepped on."

"Oh, horses are real careful of their friends. It's me I worry about getting tromped. Guess I'd better be getting on home. The old lady will be having a fit. Says I need to get me a proper job. Old Solomon don't pay much."

Brad said, "Take care. Let me know if I should bet on that colt in the Derby next May."

Jimmy was a little tipsy when Dirk followed him out of the bar, but he got into an old rusted-out truck and headed up the road to a trailer park filled with mobile homes well past their prime. Dirk noted the lot number and headed back to the motel.

The room looks a little brighter now, Dirk thought, as he sat down on the lumpy mattress with a shot of bourbon in his hand.

A different spin could be put on the situation now. Lucky he had gotten to the bar when he did; maybe fortune would smile on him this time. If the old man wanted to sell, he'd just drive right up to the barn. Nobody would recognize him after all these years. His mind now able to rest, he poured another bourbon.

Monday morning, Dirk headed for Old Solomon's place. He drove up the dirt path and beyond the fence. He gasped just before Fuzzy put some more scratches down the side of his truck. There was a red chestnut colt that reminded him of Secretariat, both in looks and actions. He had perfect legs, a sturdy barrel chest, and a star on his forehead. If this colt could run, Dirk had found his winner. Now that the hunt was over, he could cut to the chase.

He wisely stayed in his truck until Solomon called off the dog and motioned for him to roll down his window. "Help ya?" asked the old man.

"I hear you've got a colt you might be willing to part with."

Looking very wary, Solomon asked, "Where'd ya hear that?"

"Just around. Work for a fellow out in California wants a good racehorse. You interested?"

"Maybe."

"What's the breeding on the colt? He be eligible to run in the Derby next spring?"

"Yep."

"Can I look at him?"

He motioned for Dirk to get out of the truck, but the dog was still growling, and the cowboy was a little leery about opening the door. Finally, Solomon gave the dog some kind of signal, and he backed off. Dirk cautiously opened the door and stood down. Knowing that Fuzzy would recognize his scent, he proceeded with great caution, but the dog just eyed the intruder.

Dirk didn't want to appear too eager, but he knew he had to buy this colt. Jimmy was walking him to cool him down now.

"How about I come and watch his workout in the morning?" Dirk asked. "Would that be okay?"

"Yep," the old man replied. "Early. 'Bout seven."

"What's the colt's name?"

Jimmy came around with the colt about then and said, "We just call him Anonymous."

Dirk cautiously backed his body to the truck, his eyes never leaving Fuzzy as he remembered his last encounter with the huge beast. As soon as he was out of sight of the farmhouse, he floored the truck and sped back to the motel.

He hurried to his room and dialed his contact's number in California. Before it could ring, he hung up, realizing it wasn't even daylight yet on the West Coast. "Damn, better get my brain working."

Finally reaching his contact, Dirk was authorized to offer up to five million for the colt. *Guess my word's worth a lot*, he thought. The consortium wanted full ownership, though. No percentages.

Arriving at Solomon's farm the next morning at six-thirty, Dirk found Jimmy already exercising the colt, preparing for his run. Solomon arrived with Fuzzy and an old-fashioned stopwatch. At the nod of Solomon's head, Jimmy took the colt to the starting point. Anonymous sprinted at an amazing speed, almost like a quarter horse, but he just kept running faster as he ran down the straightaway toward the first curve of the makeshift track.

Dirk saw no faults in the colt. It was the most perfect horse he had ever seen. He thought, *If Anonymous can go a mile and a quarter and farther at that speed, he'll win the Triple Crown. Nobody'll be able to catch him.* Suddenly, five million seemed like cheap change.

"My boss is prepared to offer you a million dollars for your colt," Dirk said when he could speak again.

"Nope."

Jimmy couldn't believe what he was hearing. "That's a lot of money, Solomon."

"Yep."

Might as well go for the max, Dirk thought, as an evil plan began to form in his mind. "Okay," he said," I'll give you five million dollars for sole ownership of the colt. That's as high as I can go."

"Yep," said a grinning Solomon.

Dirk said he would have to get the money transferred from California. "Do you have a bank account number?"

"Yep, but I want a cashier's check," the old man said. "And the dog has to go with the colt."

"Oh, I don't know about taking the dog," said Dirk. "He doesn't seem to like me too much."

"The dog goes, or the colt stays too," Solomon said. "I'll show you how to handle him."

Jimmy explained, "The colt won't run without the dog."

"Okay," Dirk agreed. "I'll have the money sent out here."

Instead of heading back to the motel, Dirk hunted one of those facilities where he could get a box in order to receive mail. That done, he searched out a farm-type store where he thought he could find the kind of clothes Solomon wore. He was confident he could pass for the old farmer, and he found just what he needed at the store. Now it was time to call his contact to arrange for the cashier's check to be sent to his postal box and to find out where the colt was to be delivered.

They'd probably hire a trainer in Kentucky. Dirk figured if he was lucky, he'd come get the colt and the dog. Then he'd just have to get rid of Solomon Miller. He needed to think about how to accomplish that little feat, but he knew he'd have to get access to the old man's financial records first. Maybe Jimmy could be bought. He hated to kill such a young man.

It took five days for the check to get to Dirk's box. By that time, the consortium had arranged for a trainer to pick up the animals. None of them were happy about the mongrel, but Fuzzy climbed into the trailer stall next to the big colt's. Dirk had already given Solomon his check but was waiting for Jimmy to leave.

"Part of this money is yours, Jimmy," said the old man. "It'll give you a good start on your own horse farm. You deserve it."

"Thank you. You don't know how much I'll appreciate it."

After Jimmy left, Solomon looked at Dirk, obviously expecting him to take off as well.

"Pleasure doing business with you," Dirk said. "I best be on my way."

The cowboy drove down the road a ways, then returned to the farm. There was no dog to stop him now. He figured he'd finally got lucky for once in his life. All he had to do was find the checkbook. Sneaking along the side of the house, he tripped over a large rock hidden by the weeds. He almost cried out but caught himself in time. His leg was still tender, and it hurt like the devil when it hit that boulder.

Limping along, he came to a window, but the blind was closed. In fact, it seemed like all the windows were covered. "Shit," he thought. "What do I do now?"

He quietly opened the back door and slipped into the kitchen. If he got caught, he'd just have to punt. The old man was sitting at a dented metal desk with his checkbook in hand. Dirk took the cord out of his pocket, and before Solomon could react, the clothesline was tightening around his neck. With a final gasp, Solomon fell to the floor.

Now the work began. Dirk dug a grave behind the barn and wrapped the old man's body in a plastic sheet. It was tough dragging the body, but it was finally laid to rest. Dirk filled in the hole and went out to his truck to get his new clothes.

He settled into Solomon's house. The only thing he bought was a big-screen television and a satellite system. There would be enough time later to fix up the farm. He worried about how to handle Jimmy, but he didn't have any problems there. He gave Jimmy ten thousand dollars, and the young man acted like Dirk had given him a million.

"You even look like Old Solomon," he told Dirk. "I'm sorry the old fellow died from a heart attack, but I can understand about the money. Not like there are any children or anything."

Happy to have reached a settlement with the young jockey, Dirk settled in to spend the winter in southern Indiana. The consortium probably thought he had died, since he didn't return to California for his pay. His only news came from Jimmy, because Dirk was afraid to mingle with people in case they should become suspicious. The young jockey even did his grocery shopping for him.

Spring arrived with a warm breeze. Jimmy told him that Anonymous had won both the Florida and the Arkansas Derbies. The trainer felt he was ready to run for the roses.

The Kentucky Derby finally arrived. Dirk and Jimmy watched the great race on TV. The announcers compared Anonymous to the famous horses of the past, but the public must have been skeptical, because the odds were still 15 to 1 at post time.

It wasn't even a contest, though. Anonymous dominated the race. The announcers told how he had been bought from an old farmer in southern Indiana, but his registration showed he had been foaled in Louisiana by a nondescript mare and sired by a stallion that had been injured as a colt and never saw a racetrack.

It was a Cinderella story, and the press loved it. They even had a tape showing the big dog that was the colt's constant companion. They had tried to contact the farmer about the sale of the colt, but his spokesman said the old man wished to remain anonymous. Dirk looked over at Jimmy and grinned when the announcer said this.

The five owners who made up the consortium were all in the winner's circle. It was probably the first time they had even been close to the colt. Anonymous wore the roses, and everyone was talking about his winning the Triple Crown.

Dirk smirked and thought, *I don't need your million now.* He wondered if they ever thought about him or had ever tried to find him.

"Well, Jimmy, I guess you must be feeling awfully proud, since you mostly trained that colt."

"Yes, I'm feeling just great, but I need to be shopping for another colt. Just don't seem to have enough money."

"Maybe I could loan you some. Wouldn't charge you as much interest as a bank."

"That's awful nice of you, but I don't want to be in debt. How about another beer? I'm getting hungry. How about a salad and a sandwich too?"

"That sure sounds good. Want some help?"

"Nah, you watch the rest of the hoopla."

Jimmy made two salads, one of them very special. He sprinkled on some *herbs de Provence.* In Dirk's dish, he sprinkled in some crushed foxglove leaves. It would either kill him or make him sick. He didn't know how much to use. Two ham salad sandwiches, a couple of dill pickles, and some potato chips completed the meal.

"This sure is good salad, Jimmy. What did you add to make it so special?"

"Just some stuff called *herbs de Provence.* I saw one of them chefs on TV use it. I'll clean up these dishes and head on home."

About fifteen minutes later, Jimmy yelled from the kitchen to tell Dirk he was leaving.

Dirk yelled back, "You go ahead. I'm not feeling too well. Think I'll take a nap."

It was a sunny, warm day for the funeral. Several people showed up to tell Jimmy how sorry they were about Solomon's death, but said he was an old man and his heart couldn't last forever. Everyone told him how kind and generous it was of him to have a nice funeral for his friend.

Jimmy was the only mourner to drive out to the graveside services at the Miller family cemetery, but the minister he'd hired read some nice verses from the Bible and said a prayer. When it was all over, Jimmy got into his old battered truck and patted his coat pocket to make sure Solomon's will was still there. It was time to search for Derby prospects.

Juleps have been beverages since ancient times—and mint juleps were Southern thirst quenchers long before the fictional Scarlett survived the burning of Atlanta and married Rhett—but Kentucky has given the drink its international fame. For more than a century, Kentucky Derby fans have made the mint julep with Kentucky bourbon whiskey. There is even an "official mint julep" cocktail.

Little disagreement about the ingredients exists—bourbon, sugar, water, mint, and ice. And the drink is served, if possible, in silver julep cups. But wars continue each May regarding whether the sugar is granulated, powdered, or boiled into a simple syrup. Friends have become enemies over the best way to use the fresh mint. Is it boiled into syrup, refrigerated in the syrup overnight, crushed into the drink during preparation, or merely used as a garnish for a grand presentation? You decide!

Here is a simple recipe that makes one drink:

several sprigs of fresh mint

1 teaspoon sugar, either granulated or powdered

1 tablespoon water, or just enough to dissolve the sugar
crushed ice

1 or 2 jiggers premium Kentucky bourbon

Wipe the inside of a silver julep cup with a sprig of mint and discard the bruised mint. Dissolve sugar in the water in the bottom of the cup. Fill with crushed ice. Add bourbon and stir gently. Add more ice, if necessary. Garnish with a fresh sprig or two of mint. Glass tumblers can be substituted for the silver cup, but they will not frost.

Raise your cup and sip as you watch the running of the Kentucky Derby.

WIN, PLACE . . .
OR SHOW UP DEAD
by Laura Young

Laura Young, a native of Louisville, Kentucky, writes the Kate Kelly mystery series. The first book, Killer Looks, *was nominated for a 2003 Kentucky Literary Award for Fiction. Her second Kate Kelly book for Silver Dagger Mysteries is titled* Otherwise Engaged. *A former journalist, Laura covered many Kentucky Derby Festival events, and she has spent more time nosing around the press box at Churchill Downs than she should probably admit.*

THERE ARE CERTAIN rights of passage in life. There's your first bicycle, your first kiss, your first drink, your first love. There's also the accompanying score and palette that paints the backdrop of all these events. The seasons come and go but leave indelible marks in our memory banks. Every cup of hot chocolate evokes memories of the brisk winter wind from years ago, and how dreadfully long it took to unwrap the miles of scarves, gloves, and coats as Mom stood waiting with that glorious, sweet steaming concoction. Likewise, the twinkle of Christmas tree lights sends the message that gifts and good times are on the way, and the first jonquils popping out of the ground signal the imminent arrival of the Easter Bunny.

Another spring tradition that pops with the first tulips and warm afternoons is the Kentucky Derby. I know these things because I rely on calendars and events and traditions to mark my days. My name is Kate Kelly, and I'm a travel writer. My journalistic beat for *Travel Adventures*, the magazine I write for, is fun times and happy people. It sure beats covering every traffic accident, domestic dispute, and corporate scandal that rocks municipalities every day.

So, sunshine, warm weather, and great parties were what I had in mind as I bucked for an assignment to cover the Kentucky Derby this year. I'd been to the Derby before. The first time was in college when my buddies and I thought we'd be "unique" and take a road trip to Kentucky to experience the wilds of the Churchill Downs infield. We were hardly unique as we joined thousands of sunburned, drunken revelers. I never saw a horse that day, but it was certainly memorable.

Equally memorable was two years ago when I received the plum work assignment to cover Millionaires Row for *Travel Adventures.* I still never saw a horse that day, but I did manage to drink a mint julep with Dixie Carter, trade betting tips with Danny DeVito, and have my posterior pinched by Prince Albert of Monaco.

I thought it would be a wonderful idea to return to Millionaires Row again this year, but in their infinite wisdom, my editors decided to look at another side of the Derby. The side that most travelers don't see. The backside. At dawn. Otherwise known to sleepy Louisvillians as Dawn at the Downs.

I laughed at first. Surely they jested. Anyone remotely knowledgeable about me knows that I don't do dawn. Not at all.

"It will be good for you," my editor said. "You'll see how the other half lives. There *is* life before lunch, you know."

He could be such a comedian. In other words, I had my assignment and marching orders.

* * *

Before I left, I did my research, as any good reporter does. It wasn't that difficult, and I had plenty of reading material. There were a few national AP stories about the exorbitant cost of a Saudi prince's equine entourage, and a scandal involving horses in Florida with sponges up their noses, but the thought of foreign objects jammed up anyone's nose—horse or human—brought back bad memories of my visit to a sinus specialist a while back, so I skipped those stories.

I scoured press clips to learn the faces and names. Joe Parina and G. Dodd Keller, famous trainers and bitter rivals, had arrived on site from California and were instant media darlings. The early favorite was a horse named Bayou Folly.

A grizzly old guy named Scooter, who hangs out at the bus stop near my apartment every day, gave me an impromptu education in bloodlines and betting. I learned the local lingo and hot spots.

The great myth around the world is that the Kentucky Derby lasts only one day. In reality, it's a raucous party for more than two weeks as Louisville nearly shuts down for a full-tilt extravaganza of fun. I arrived early in the week and found plenty of things to keep me occupied from dawn until well past dusk. Everywhere I went, from the Victorian bed and breakfast I called home in Old Louisville, to the corn dog, elephant ear, and beer-laden Chow Wagons, people were instant experts in horse racing lore. They also were apparently intimate with many of the famous folks descending on Louisville, since they spoke on a first-name basis with absolute authority on where Demi or Mel or Princess So-and-So was partying that evening.

Since I had such an early wake-up call, I missed most of the celebrity sightings. Instead, I counted the stars in the sky while a very sleepy cab driver took me to Churchill Downs at 4:45 A.M. Churchill Downs' magnificent twin spires greeted me in the dark, and a serene calm floated over the predawn air as I checked in at the gate with my media credentials. In just a few hours, this peaceful, historical monument would be awash in thousands of revelers anxious to get in the Derby spirit a few days early.

My job required me to go where others do, so I immediately searched through the darkened backside for the first tent glowing with light. It was bustling at this early hour with track employees, trainers, jockeys, and media, feasting on Krispy Kreme doughnuts, fruit, and coffee. Like everyone else, I ignored the fruit and grabbed a couple of chocolate-covered doughnuts.

"So, the way I hear it," I overheard a photographer gleefully announce, "was that he looked over, pointed to her, and said, 'I will have her by day's end.'"

I noticed the naughty giggles that followed weren't from a group of 13-year-old boys, but from a collection of adults who should have known better.

"And the next thing you know," he continued breathlessly, "she was being dropped off places in the wee hours from a stretch limo. I work with her. She drives a '95 Escort. She's not a limo girl, but when you're doing research like *that,* well, I guess things change."

Laughter erupted again, and I smiled as if I understood the joke. I moved over to the coffee carafes and filled a Styrofoam cup to the brim. Nearby, a cluster of jockeys spoke in low tones.

Martino Albiero, a jockey so famous even I recognized him, spoke intently to his colleagues in broken English. "The man, he's messing with destiny. My destiny. I tell him, this gets out? You, me, we're *finito.* How you throw so much away for that? What about his family? I'm an honorable man. I don't believe in such actions."

The jockeys nodded solemnly. One spotted me listening, then turned his back to me. "Look at them," he said, jerking a thumb in my direction. "They know. They listen. It's all they talk about. It's bad for us, bad for the industry. I hate that man's ability to bring our profession to its knees like this. He should be stopped."

Albiero crushed his empty coffee cup. "And, I must do that. I must risk the consequences."

Another jockey snorted. "Not if Nightingale gets to him first. He thought he'd be the one to ride Rolling Stone, not you."

Even though several sets of eyes burned holes through the press pass hanging from a ribbon around my neck, I tried nonchalantly to study the crowd as if I was blissfully unaware of their conversation. However, my springtime hay fever tradition kicked in suddenly, and I collapsed into a sneezing fit that would wake the dead. The jockeys, apparently thinking I had the plague, frowned and scattered. Albiero, though, snapped a paper napkin from a metal holder and handed it to me.

"Stuffy nose?" he asked. "It's a terrible thing, isn't it, not to be able to breathe clearly? I understand that. Nothing and no one should be subject to that, no?"

Ah, he might be a famous jockey, but he was a fellow allergy sufferer like boring old me.

"No, I don't suppose they should," I replied. "Thanks for the tissue."

Albiero shook his head and walked away. "No one and nothing. It's not right."

I hung around the tent a few more minutes but didn't learn much more. I decided it would be prudent to figure out an angle for my story—and actually get to work. I left the doughnuts behind and searched out my allotted workspace.

Print reporters are relegated to the basement of the nearby Derby Museum. The good news is that you're safe from the elements on cold, wet mornings while you bang out your stories on laptop computers. The bad news is that you're isolated from the action, which is why you're there in the first place.

My story was on the backside, not in the basement. I decided to camp out by the TV sets and watch the morning shows in action. It was a circus under spotlights. While stars still twinkled, artificial daylight glowed, as unnaturally perky reporters acted truly excited to be awake at such an ungodly hour. I pulled my jacket tighter around me and used my *Daily Racing Form* to scrape mud off my shoes.

I watched for a while but quickly lost interest because all I could hear were the lead-ins to stories and the peppy banter that led to commercial breaks. The actual news stories all ran on air in some distant live truck, to the delight of morning viewers at home but oblivious to people watching in person.

The TV people really have the best of the backside, although to hear them tell it, you'd never believe it. Each station has a mini set, built back-to-back along the paddock area. It's convenient for the satellite trucks and technicians, who can plop miles of cable in areas where the Churchill patrons are safe but the legions of reporters and photographers are prone to tripping and breaking bones at every step. The sets have appropriately Derbyish backdrops, but the barstool anchor chairs sink into the grassy muck that covers the paddock area. Thank heaven for the tight shots that focus on the neatly coifed and suited anchors and ignore the mud-covered shoes that clomped through the paddock at the break of dawn.

The most exciting thing that happened was the apparent disappearance of one station's female anchor. I saw Tiffany Birmingham saunter off the set while the weather and sports guys took over for an extended period, but time was ticking. A hulk of a bearded director wearing a headset thundered past, booming demands to "Find her! I don't care who she's with! She's working, she can play later! Find her, now!"

I finished my coffee and tossed the cup in a trash can, thinking, *Hey, here's my television break*. I could run up, take over Tiffany's seat, and save the day. How hard could it be? But my TV debut would have to wait. About thirty feet ahead, Tiffany Birmingham and Joe Parina emerged from behind a live truck, deep in conversation. Aha, the gossip I'd heard that morning made more sense. Could this be the whispered couple?

Tiffany was impossibly tall and rail thin, with a delicately chiseled face that would make Parisian runway photographers swoon. Her willowy figure was disgustingly perfect and crowned with a flowing mass of brick-red curls that never frizzed and never fell out of place. Word had it that women wanted to be her. Men simply wanted her.

I wouldn't normally consider Parina a "catch." He was a head shorter than Tiffany and had an unremarkable face. He wasn't a snappy dresser at the moment, either. His boots and cream chinos were blotched with mud that matched the color of his leather jacket. The bright color, though, came with his trademark hair, which bordered on dayglow orange. A roadmap of bright freckles traversed across his pale skin. He wasn't exactly Adonis.

But he had millions in bank accounts, and a reported lethal ability to charm with a craggy, husky voice. Undoubtedly, the checkbook balance, limousines, and weekends flying off in private jets to the Caribbean raised his stakes dramatically in the romance department. His wife and kids were surely mere inconveniences to be dealt with at a future date.

Moments later, a disheveled Tiffany ran back on the set. The stretch run was rough, given the mud on her panty hose and clumps caked on her three-inch heels. She tossed her purse on the ground, but it landed haphazardly, and makeup, brushes, sponges, tweezers, and a bottle of hair spray poured out. Uttering an unladylike expletive, she shoved the contents back inside the purse, then jumped in her chair and furiously tapped the mud off her heels.

In the spirit of media camaraderie, I walked to the edge of the set and offered her a tissue from my purse. She glared at me and turned away, only to explode into a dazzling smile seconds later as the floor director cued her.

So much for that. I retreated over to a paddock fence out of the way of prima donna anchors. The sports guy stood nearby, his head buried in assorted sports sections, racing forms, and racing stat sheets.

I leaned against the fence. "Hi. Mind if I join you? I'm Kate Kelly. I'm a reporter for *Travel Adventures.*"

He obviously wasn't a fan of the magazine. The blank stare said a mouthful. He recovered quickly and smiled broadly. "Justin Tyme, Channel 23." He extended his hand. "I'm sure you've seen the awful promos—'Just in Time Sports With Justin Tyme'? I've complained to the station's general manager and just about anyone else who will listen."

"That is pretty awful," I agreed. I decided to make a friend. "Is there some sort of intrigue going on around the backside here? Everyone was buzzing in the press tent."

Justin shoved his newspaper into a blazer pocket. "You're kidding me, right? This is the track. Intrigue is *huge* here. It's what keeps it and the media going 24/7."

He smiled and waved an accusing finger at me. "Where did you say you're from? You're baiting me on purpose because I work with her, aren't you? Listen, it's not a scoop. This has been going on for months. Happens all the time, actually. Big money, famous trainers, girls old enough to be their daughters but don't know any better. Oldest story in the world. Joe Public doesn't know about it, and quite frankly, they probably couldn't care less. You know how incestuous the media family is, though. We love this stuff."

He patted my elbow. "Keep it within the family, Kate. No one else cares. Look, nice chatting with you, but I go on air in four minutes. Find another story to cover."

Not too many minutes later, I did have another story to cover. A plaintive wail wafted through the TV area, causing everyone to look up, but when nothing else happened immediately, work resumed.

Moments later, the wail was followed by a scream that definitely caught everyone's attention. The source came from a small barn in the back of the paddock. Track employees began running from all directions, and when we saw the off-duty Louisville policeman who was pulling Derby duty sprint past, gun drawn, we *all* took notice.

The first race of the day began, as a pack of journalists, myself included, rounded the turn, leapt over television cables, and played hopscotch over sets, all trying to get to the barn. We clambered around the barn's entrance, but there wasn't much to see. A stall door was ajar; and, haphazardly scattered, odiferous mounds of horse manure were piled in lumps. On the largest mound, a jockey's silk cap and riding whip crowned the pile. Creative, perhaps, but the kicker was the foot sticking out of one edge of the manure. Frantic digging would soon reveal its owner, but the racing cap and a head count confirmed the distraught whispers. Martino Albiero had competed in his last race.

And he came in dead last.

Literally.

Police descended on the scene in warp speed, and a grim-faced Joe Parina led Albiero's nervous Derby mount, Rolling Stone, to another barn. No sense in further spooking a multimillion-dollar investment just days before the Derby. While the police investigation got under way, the call to the post hit the airwaves, and word spread faster than a $7 mint julep sliding down the throat of an infield regular.

Churchill Downs exploded in a frenzy of media coverage, curious onlookers, and armchair detectives as the day went on. Rumors and innuendo were the immediate favorites, with accusations following a close third. Parina and G. Dodd Keller were spotted in a violent shouting match. Roses piled up in front of the police-tape-draped barn in an impromptu memorial for Albiero. Jockeys cried, then lined up to talk to the police and point fingers.

And, as the day went on, most fingers were pointed squarely at Parina.

Stories reigned about his desire to win the Derby at any cost. My morning conversation with Albiero came back to haunt me as talk of Parina's plan to find someone like Albiero to sponge the noses of Rolling Stone's rival horses surfaced. Sponges cut down on a racehorse's ability to breathe, depriving the animal of oxygen and slowing it down. Churchill Downs officials immediately held an afternoon press conference and insisted that Parina's plan would never have worked because track officials examine horses' nostrils with an endoscope before each race.

Regardless, more accusations flew, including other sinister plans to drug Rolling Stone into a frenzy as the Derby began, and talk of payoffs to other jockeys to purposely slow their horses in the stretch run, allowing Rolling Stone to overtake them. Parina angrily denied every charge, and by the afternoon, he was turning the tables and accusing poor Albiero of threatening to poison the feed of other horses. It was hard to know whom to believe, and worried Churchill Downs brass immediately ordered a check of all horse feed on the track.

Police decided to play it safe as well. In a spectacularly timed swoop that was caught by the scores of cameras on the property, the police arrested Parina under suspicion of murder. They paraded him through the paddock—not as protection for a rich, famous trainer, but as a criminal being led to jail.

Before horses rounded the far turn in the ninth race of the day, Parina had traded his private jets for a private jail cell. His empire fell under minute scrutiny, and that night on the news, the boys at the Thoroughbred Racing Commission frowned dourly. Evidence mounted almost hourly, from the veterinarian's inspections of the other horses, to the discovery of sponging material in the trunk of Parina's Jaguar, to chatty conversations with other jockeys eager to defend the honor of a fallen colleague.

Joe Parina was turning out to be more like Joe Pariah. He was vilified throughout prime time and with enough ink to cover reams of newspapers. The clincher came when police announced the damning evidence of strands of red hair embedded in the manure clinging to part of a shovel used to bury Albiero.

It looked like an open-and-shut case. The whole torrid affair still hummed around the track and area newsrooms, but most Louisvillians promptly shoved the story away and continued with the week-long party. It would make great "So, what didya think about" conversation over many a cookout in the coming days, but Derby enthusiasts knew what really mattered—the fastest two minutes in sports.

On Derby Day, they got what they wanted. Rolling Stone made an early break out of the gate but soon faded with a new, unfamiliar jockey aboard. Instead, Parina's rival, G. Dodd Keller, breezed into the winner's circle. As he accepted the trophy and blanket of roses from the governor, he made an impassioned speech about the integrity of his stables and the importance of upholding the proud traditions that make the Kentucky Derby a grand event. A network commentator wondered aloud if Parina was watching the show from his jail cell.

The Derby was over. Planning blissfully began for next year's festivities. Justin Tyme was correct—the intrigue was all just part of the game.

So, you see, sometimes eavesdropping isn't that bad of a hobby. You can quietly soak up all kinds of information. Tawdry affairs of the heart. Dirty backside deals. Million-dollar gossip. Little things mean a big deal. Gaining all that information is kind of like being a big sponge. You never know what you're going to soak up.

With her scandalous affair out in the open, one would think Tiffany Birmingham would disappear into the media shadows. However, she was front and center, bravely smiling at the camera. She even showed up at Parina's arraignment the Monday after the Derby, clad in Jackie O. sunglasses, with a silk scarf wrapped around her red curls.

While all the cameras chased after Parina and his attorney, I headed for Tiffany. I tried the tissue approach once more, and this time, she took it.

"Thanks," she said hoarsely as she pulled off her sunglasses and dabbed her eyes.

"Why did you do it, Tiffany?" I said.

Her eyes grew to the size of fried eggs, and the color drained from her face. A rumble began in her toes and rolled up in a wave through her whole body. "How did you know? I never meant for it to happen. But he was going to ruin Joe's life. Joe knew what he was doing; he had a plan. We were going to win the Derby. But Albiero wouldn't agree to the sponging. No one had to know. Joe was paying him an enormous amount of money, so why couldn't he keep his mouth shut? They had a terrible argument. I overheard it, and Albiero started threatening Joe, saying he was going to Churchill officials and was going to tell all. Then he started saying really nasty things about me and my relationship with Joe. I love Joe. I would do anything for him."

She sank into a doorway for support, and the tears flowed freely. "When Joe stormed out, Albiero just went back to working around Rolling Stone as if nothing had happened. Something just overtook me. I went back to our truck and got a tripod, and I ran in there and just swung it at him." Tiffany shuddered. "He went down immediately. I knew he was dead. I was frantic—angry, scared—I didn't know what to do. I couldn't drag his body anywhere, so I started shoveling manure on top of him. I thought that was appropriate, given all he had said to Joe. I guess I just snapped."

Certainly seemed to be the case.

Lucky for me, but bad for Tiffany, she hadn't noticed the sheriff's deputy standing near us. He apparently liked to eavesdrop, too. He quickly joined our conversation, and life slid downhill immediately for Tiffany. Within minutes, I had an exclusive and she was wearing handcuffs.

Later, as I finished my final call to the LPD homicide division and typed the last paragraph of my story, I stared at my laptop screen. It wasn't the typical story I write for *Travel Adventures,* but it sure was a doozy.

And all thanks to Tiffany. How could she have known that all I was really asking her was why she became Parina's mistress? I never expected the answer I got instead. Tiffany Birmingham threw away a promising career, prestige, glamour, and the rest of her life for a guy who had the morals of a horseshoe.

I had trouble comprehending the reasons why, so I left the computer and switched on the television. The evening news was just coming on, and the promo leading the newscast trumpeted "Hell hath no fury!" as a split screen showed a triumphant Parina being released from jail, Armani suit intact, and a brutal close-up of Tiffany's tear-stained cheeks and mascara-smudged raccoon eyes.

As video rolled of her being led away in handcuffs, yet another impossibly thin and beautiful anchor breathlessly led the news that evening: "Our big story tonight. . . .

TAKE A STAB AT THESE MYSTERIES COMING SOON

Reporter Kate Kelly masquerades as a friend's fiancée for a weekend adventure at a beautiful Kentucky horse farm. But when a deadly explosion rocks the farm, Kate quickly learns that planning a wedding involves more than wearing a huge diamond ring and picking out china patterns. It might just be the death of her.

Otherwise Engaged

by
Laura Young

Beans, Boots, and Bullets

by
Daniel Bailey

Storm clouds threaten South Carolina, but the hurricane off the coast of Charleston isn't the turbulence to be feared. As the Presidential election nears, a political storm brews, churned by a militant militia seeking anarchy and financed by a renegade band of corporate powerbrokers determined to control the White House.

If Williamsburg shop owner Emma Spencer wants to live, she has to find out why someone wants her dead. Her investigation ranges from the swamps of South Carolina to a deserted farm in Virginia, and Emma uncovers more than anyone expected: family secrets, an old murder, and deadly connections.

Death by Any Other Name

by
Ellis Vidler

SILVER DAGGER MYSTERIES